PENGUIN CRIME FICTION

MURDOCK FOR HIRE

Robert J. Ray was born in Amarillo, Texas; earned a doctorate in English at the University of Texas in Austin; taught English for thirteen years and tennis for five years; and now lives in Irvine, California, where he teaches fiction writing at Irvine Valley College. Mr. Ray's previous novel, *Bloody Murdock* (Penguin), was the first Matt Murdock mystery. He is the author of two other novels, *The Heart of the Game* and *Cage of Mirrors*.

MURDOCK FOR HIRE

Robert J. Ray

Penguin Books

PENGUIN BOOKS
Published by the Penguin Group
Viking Penguin Inc., 40 West 23rd Street,
New York, New York 10010, U.S.A.
Penguin Books Ltd, 27 Wrights Lane, London W8 5TZ, England
Penguin Books Australia Ltd, Ringwood,
Victoria, Australia
Penguin Books Canada Limited, 2801 John Street,
Markham, Ontario, Canada L3R 1B4
Penguin Books (N.Z.) Ltd, 182–190 Wairau Road,
Auckland 10, New Zealand

Penguin Books Ltd, Registered Offices:
Harmondsworth, Middlesex, England

First published in the United States of America by
St. Martin's Press 1987
Reprinted by arrangement with St. Martin's Press, Inc.
Published in Penguin Books 1988

This is a work of fiction. Any resemblance of any characters
to any person, living or dead, is purely coincidental.

LIBRARY OF CONGRESS CATALOGING IN PUBLICATION DATA
Ray, Robert J. (Robert Joseph), 1935–
Murdock for hire.
(Penguin crime fiction)
I. Title.
[PS3568.A9218M8   1988]   813'.54   87-7163
ISBN 0 14 01.0679 0

Printed in the United States of America by
Offset Paperback Mfrs., Inc., Dallas, Pennsylvania
Set in Baskerville

ACKNOWLEDGMENTS

Some very good people helped shape *Murdock for Hire*. I got excellent advice on rough drafts from Jean Femling, from Bill and Sharon Wood, from Dan Logan, from my eager students in the fiction workshop at Irvine Valley College, and from the ever-sagacious writers of the Orange County Fictionaires.

Jay Styron helped me assemble Murdock's arsenal.

Roger Angle gave me the title.

Jared Kieling, my super editor at St. Martin's, helped balance the final draft.

Maureen Walters, my agent at Curtis Brown, believed in Murdock early.

And my wife, Margot, encouraged me by urging: "Hit those keys."

This book is for all of them.

MURDOCK
FOR HIRE

PROLOGUE

When the hookers fluttered in, Eddie Hennessy was standing at the bar, drinking his second Dewar's on the rocks while he talked shop with Barney Ratner, his marketing vice president. Eddie felt edgy, beat from twelve hours at the office, and the sight of a dozen pretty girls cheered him up.

How did Barney Ratner do it? He was at his desk at six. He charged through the day, making deals, grinning with confidence, putting away two martinis at lunch, and still emerged sharp and ready for battle after work. Ratner's khaki suit had no creases. His tie was still tight. His name tag said Mr. Black.

"Hey! Hey!" Ratner said. "Here comes the parade."

Eddie drank some Dewar's. He wanted to loosen his tie and unbutton his collar button. The shirt, a blue oxford cloth from Brooks Brothers, had been a birthday gift from his daughter, two years ago. It was a great shirt. His Florsheims pinched his feet.

"There's your dream girl, Mr. Black. Number Six."

Ratner bopped Eddie's bicep. "Miss Steam Heat of Newport Beach. I can taste the honey from here."

"She fakes her moans, for Christ's sake."

"They sound real enough to me, boss."

Now the hookers fluttered into the fifth-floor suite at the Cote D'Azur like tropical birds—tangerine dress, turquoise dress, white beads, slender arms, shining hair—and Eddie's heart beat faster. He was forty-nine years old and thirty pounds overweight. He owned his own company, EJH Designs. His last contract with the air force had grossed $43 million for software development. Tonight, Eddie and the hookers would become history, and he wanted a new girl, one he knew but didn't know.

Now disappointment soured him as the hookers fanned out into the room and Eddie saw no one new. They were pretty, with curvy bodies and sharp college-girl faces. They were clean, quick-witted, adventurous in bed. None of them turned him on. Then he spotted her, a bright-eyed redhead with long legs and a valentine face. Eddie caught her eye and smiled. She smiled back. What would her number be? How would she look in the mask?

Then Tommy Talbot, Eddie's neighbor in Turtle Rock, came up wearing his Mr. Blue name tag. "Hey, you hackers. We still on for Saturday?" Tommy was lean and handsome. Fifteen years ago, he'd played a year on the international tennis circuit. Rome. Paris. Gstaad. Wimbledon. Eddie had always wanted to take a year off and just play. He envied Tommy.

Ratner faked a punch that barely missed Tommy's nose. "Your ass is mud, buddy boy."

At that moment, indigestion rumbled inside Eddie and he felt the heaviness of pain. He drank some Dewar's,

2

then nodded at Tommy and grinned. "Mr. Black talks big, but we know who's got the shots."

Ratner grinned his competitor's grin, then spoke to Tommy. "Tell us, Mr. Blue. How's the insurance game? Soft as ever? Ready for some real competition?"

"We welcome competition, Mr. Black. Try me anytime."

Ratner laughed.

Eddie felt sick. It was August, and Eddie had been bickering with Ratner since April about where to look for future customers for EJH Designs. Ratner wanted more contracts with the air force, the army, the Department of Defense. Eddie disagreed because Washington was already their major customer. Defense cutbacks would start the minute a new president took over in Washington. The Pentagon had just lopped off Winslow Instrumentation, causing three hundred layoffs. Eddie didn't want the ax to fall on EJH Designs. His dream was to supply user-friendly software for the business community. EJH Designs was his shop, started in his garage and then built on luck and midnight sweat. Let the Pentagon business be forty percent, certainly no more than fifty.

The blonde, Number 6, waved. Ratner shrugged his massive shoulders, then moved away, his powerful body thrusting toward his target. He spoke over his shoulder. "See you Saturday, buddy boys. Bring money."

"If you skip down to Rosarita," Tommy called, "let us know, so we can dredge up a real fourth."

Ratner answered with a clenched fist.

Eddie stood with Tommy at the bar, monitoring his indigestion. Across the room, the redhead caught his eye and threw him a smile. He hefted his glass in a toast and smiled back.

He was talking insurance premiums with Tommy when Number 12, the manager, came up to introduce the new redhead. Her nameplate, gold letters on glossy white, read NUMBER 18. He'd seen numbers as high as thirty-seven at the Monday mixers. How many girls worked Lido Enterprises? Where did they come from? How were they trained?

Eddie was a businessman, an entrepreneur. He was always fascinated by secrets of the trade.

"Mr. Brown, Mr. Blue, I'd like to introduce Number Eighteen."

She was prettier up close, lights highlighting her coppery hair. Cool green eyes surveyed him. Like the others, she had healthy skin, straight teeth, a middle-American, middle-class look. What was her real name? What would he call her? What would she look like wearing the mask?

Tommy excused himself. "See you Saturday, partner. We'll clean the court with those clowns." And then, to Number 18: "Nice meeting you."

"Likewise, Mr. Blue." The redhead shook hands with Tommy before he moved off.

"You're new." Jeanette? Janie? Julie?

"Yes. I just arrived. From out of town." She widened the smile, moved closer. "You're cute."

That made him blush. "Hey. Men aren't 'cute.'"

She took his arm in both hands. "The other girls say you're really nice, Mr. Brown. The nicest one, they said." Her closeness turned him on. One of the rules at the Monday mixers was no hanky-panky. No kissing, no fondling asses, no rough stuff. Lust touched him and he was helpless, as if he was a kid again, back in St. Louis. The girl's eyes widened.

"You all right?"

4

"Sure. It's just that . . . you're so darn beautiful."

"Why, thank you, Mr. Brown. What a sweet thing to say."

He shifted gears. "How long have you been—down here."

"Oh, three weeks." She was offhand. "A month."

"Just came back from the wine country myself. Little trip. This is my first night back." He meant the Cote D'Azur, the Monday mixer. "Ever been up to the wine country?"

"Oh, sure. When I lived in the Bay Area, we—" Number 18 stopped, blushed, put her hand to her mouth. "Gosh, I almost blew it. Don't tell Number Twelve, okay?"

Eddie grinned. Her vulnerability made him feel strong. "Your secret is safe with me."

"Gosh. Thanks."

Desire mushroomed inside him as they talked. Heart thundering, he lost himself in her green eyes, a moment of escape, the cobweb rhythms of seduction. He felt unsightly, like a great toad. He gulped the rest of his Dewar's. She took his glass, mixed him another.

The fresh drink balanced him, man on the edge. More and more, he lived there, teetering. The redhead displayed her Club Lido training and kept the talk neutral—sports and the weather, movies, her trip to Chicago, her fear of being hijacked. She was less sympathetic about the airline strike than he was.

The hour was up. Time to plan Hennessy's last ride. "Wednesday afternoon? You and me?"

As he waited for her answer, he was still the edgy fat kid from St. Louis.

At last she nodded. "Love to." They made a date for

5

Wednesday afternoon. She handed him her Lido Enterprises business card. It had raised gold letters, an Old English script on white gloss. There was no address, just her number, 18, and a local phone with the area code omitted. "In case you change your mind."

"Not a chance."

Number 18 squeezed his hand. When she left the room with the others, he felt empty.

The boys of the South Bay Executive Network had one for the road. They discussed the prime, employees asleep on the job, bank factoring at forty-seven percent on the dollar. Insurance premiums were climbing. Everyone wanted a Republican in the White House. After the meeting, he walked out with Ratner.

"Seven more guys called me this week. They want in."

Eddie didn't care. He was leaving the SBEN. But he fought Ratner out of habit. "We're too big now, Barney."

"Treasury could use the initiation fees."

"As fellow founder, I'd have to say no."

"Buddy boy, if you weren't my boss, I'd toss your butt in the hotel fish pond."

"We're overgrown, Barn. If word about us got out—"

Ratner grabbed his arm. "This is candy, Eddie. I've been strategizing an SBEN franchise. A chapter in every city over two hundred thousand. One percent of that, we could kiss the air force good-bye! And the DOD!"

Eddie was tired of Ratner's schemes. Working with Ratner used to be good. Now it made his head feel like fuzz balls from a vacuum cleaner bag. They rode the elevator down to street level and went through a side door. Outside, in the August twilight, the Cote D'Azur parking lot was heavy with hot white smog. Lights winked on, preparing this part of California for darkness. On Pacific

Coast Highway, traffic shuffled by. Ratner unlocked the door of his black Mercedes, then made some locker room predictions of his upcoming date with the blonde, Number 6. Ratner was divorced and a couple of years younger.

"See you tomorrow," Eddie said. "Eight-thirty briefing with those software people. My office."

"Read you, buddy boy."

Driving home, he envied Barney. No clinging wife. All the world for a playpen.

Next day at the office, Eddie's secretary cleared his calendar for Wednesday afternoon, and he phoned the Lido Enterprise number to confirm, using his Mr. Brown code name. The pickup was at Casere's on Coast Highway at three o'clock. He would pay cash. That meant a trip to the bank.

Wednesday morning, he withdrew a thousand in cash out of his Wells Fargo account. In the Porsche, he counted the stack, twenty fifties, stiff, smelling new. Only $1,595 left in this account. The radio said London gold was up eight dollars from yesterday. He drove to Barclays, opened his safety-deposit box, pulled out his coin collection. If gold rose four dollars tomorrow, he'd sell the lot for $550,000 and EJH Designs would be out of the woods.

Back at the office in the Irvine Industrial Complex, he locked the coins in his private safe, behind the suits and spare shirts in the closet. The cocaine sat there in the plastic envelope with the slide closure. It was like a sandwich bag and it reminded him of his brown bag days, before EJH Designs, when he'd worked for the big corporations back East. These were better times. But he missed his wife's sandwiches.

At two-thirty Wednesday afternoon, Eddie left the office and headed southwest toward Newport Beach. The summer traffic was heavy. Waiting in the gridlock made him sweat, so he turned up the air in the Porsche. Off to his left, the yacht harbor slid by in sultry motion, sailboats drifting along, and he thought about the weekend, taking the *Laredo II* out for a sail. He'd ask Christine. Maybe she'd have a change of heart. Or maybe Lizzie would come down from her seminar at Santa Barbara.

At Casere's, waiting for the redhead, he ignored the warnings of Dr. Hunsaker and ordered Budweiser on draft. It was cool and bitter going down. He couldn't think of a present for Lizzie's birthday. Last year, he'd given her the Toyota. This year, he was giving up sin.

The door to the steamy parking lot opened when he was midway through the second Bud and Number 18 stood silhouetted in a bleak rectangle of afternoon sunlight. Watching her long legs outlined by the fierce brightness behind her made Eddie's mouth dry. That was what the beer was for.

He met her halfway and took her arm. She smiled, seeming to sense how hot he was for her. When she saw the Porsche in the lot, she smiled again.

"Oh, a Targa! Please, can I drive?"

Against his better judgment, he said okay.

She wheeled the brown Targa down Pacific Coast Highway, past Le Club on the right, Reuben's, Baxter's, the sails on the water, up the hill, the sun bright and harsh, a shift of gears and her skirt opening, showing a lot of leg, revving his motor, making him catch his breath as she hit the clutch to slow for the stoplight at Mac-Arthur, and then on through Corona del Mar, where

Christine had her eye on a house, $882,000 and change, and southeast down the highway to Laguna.

"You're a helluva driver, Number Eighteen."

"Thanks, Mr. Brown." She put a hand on his thigh.

A mile from the center of Laguna, Number 18 turned left off Coast Highway and headed into the hills. Knocka-doon Road, steep and winding. The slit in the white skirt was wider now. His wife had a skirt that same color, only with cloth-covered buttons. He felt light-headed and blamed the heat, the two beers. She turned a tight corner, throwing him against the door. Up ahead, the Bougaine-ville. She parked in the same reserved slot, leaned side-ways, grabbed him behind the neck, and stuck her tongue in his mouth. He groped at her. She pulled away, breath-ing hard, hand on her bosom.

"I have to ask for it. House rules."

He handed her the fifties, which she shoved into her purse. They used the back entrance, a heavy orange metal door that she unlocked with a key from a giant ring.

In the elevator, going up, he felt woozy.

It was the same corner suite, number 611, looking southwest to the Pacific. The air-conditicning hummed. On a table by the window was a magnum of regulation Dom Perignon in a silver ice bucket. On the south wall, an X-rated movie rolled across a jumbo-sized TV screen. He brought out the coke. They each did a line. He felt it lift him up, boost his spirits. Man power. The hooker was ready for him, smiling.

After the first blast-off, they showered together, gig-gling, frolicking like kids. Watching her body, slick under the spray, he marveled once more at the wasted magic of youth. After tonight, his last ride, he would go on a diet, cut down on the booze, play more tennis, jog, drop some lard. There were two smart-ass kids at the Irvine Racquet Club who called him the Old Fart. He would trim down and nail them both. His mind bounced happily between great ideas. How would it be to divorce Christine, marry Number 18, and sail the *Laredo II* to Tahiti? How would it be to fire Barney Ratner?

Drying off, he spotted his gold wedding band, then slowly removed it when the hooker wasn't looking. They climbed back into bed. He'd paid for paradise. This was it—coke, silky sex, ultimate possession—and he heard himself screaming in primal release.

She brought champagne to the bed. "You were great, Mr. Brown."

"Tell me your name."

"Sorry."

"I'll christen you. Jeanette. Julie. Jane. Jan." He splashed her with champagne. "Julie. Janey. Jan."

"Okay, Jeanette. I like."

They sipped, slowly, the cool fizz sewing a silver fringe on the afternoon. A couple of beakers of bubbly, another line, and he was ready for the big cavalry charge. They experimented with positions for pleasure—pilot to copilot, how's this from the *Kama Sutra*? And this? If only the wife could see him, galloping along the edge, balanced between ecstasy and oblivion.

He fell asleep wondering about the mask.

It was twilight when he woke. Number 18 was gone from the bed. He felt unsteady sitting up. The TV screen was blank. He heard a soft hum, a mechanical whirring. "Hey, Jean! Hey, Jeanie!"

The whirlies hit him again as he swung his legs over

10

the side of the bed, seeing his white feet, the tennis tan. He popped open a beer from the fridge, loaded a slice of steak with Mexi-Pep. Since he was a kid in St. Louis, he'd loved hot sauce on red meat. Was that part of his customer profile at Club Lido? Code Name: Mr. Brown. Age: 49. Income: six figures. Car: Porsche, leased, $47,750. Residence: Irvine, $367,000. Tastes: steak, hot sauce, cocaine. Needs: to live on the edge and not fall. Toys: Mac 512K; yacht, *Laredo II;* sassy hookers; S & M; gold coins. Hobbies: tennis; secret poetry.

His wife hated cold steak.

The door opened six inches and one black boot snaked into view. Spike heel, gleaming leather. "Jeanette, remember?"

"Sorry. Jeanette. I was never good with names."

And then the door opened all the way and she appeared. The black boots went halfway up her brazen thighs, buccaneer style. On top, a vest of black leather, one size too small, decorated with silver chains. On her hands, long black gloves. In her right hand, she carried the leather mask.

He trembled now.

She hid the mask behind her back and knelt beside him on the bed. "I am the guide."

She snatched the beer can from him and threw it aside. Thump, against the wall. She emptied champagne on him. He squirmed. On to the other world.

She straddled him smiling, and he heard the soft whirring sound to his left and looked over at the TV. The TV screen was still blank.

"Oooh," she said, taking him.

Riding the edge was what it was all about. Riding the edge in business, in life, in bed. He saw spirals, vortices, a gathering maelstrom. He knew this maelstrom. It was the symbol of his big-money breakthrough for the air force. Make software for the air force to finance your home in paradise, to fulfill the promise of California.

Teetering on the divide, Eddie felt a tiny warning pain in the chest, zapping his right shoulder. A red light burned above the bed. Outside, darkness had sucked up the sun.

"Do you want the mask?"

Her face was in shadow as he pulled her down, touched her face, smooth leather. In the spooky red light, she stared at him through yellow Velcro eyes. The masked hooker and the great toad. Suddenly, the pain in his chest blossomed, bombing his pleasure, and he clawed at the mask.

"Tell me you want it!" she whispered. "Beg!"

Eddie wanted her off his chest, so he could breathe. He wanted to know her goddamn name. An insect buzzed. The toad inside him flicked a red tongue. Light blazed behind his eyeballs. There was a stone on his chest, crushing him, squeezing, pressing home the fear. He tried to throw the girl off, thinking illusion, cash flow, Velcro face, room to breathe, buttons on white skirts, brown Porsche, Number 18, Barney Ratner, software for the air force, wife and daughter, birthday, wages of sin, and then the mask on her face turned into a huge pair of black wings that closed around his ears, shutting out the world, and he was dead.

1

What do you do when one of your co-owners dies?

What steps do you take when you sink $10,000 into a boat that cost $110,000 and the angry widow of a recently deceased co-owner wants to sell her $55,000 share and you don't have the money to buy her out?

You think about the problem. You drink cold beer. You lose yourself in detail work.

It was ninety in the shade that August day at the Bay Avenue dock, a sweatbox condition known in California as a Santa Ana. In a Santa Ana, the cool ocean breezes die down, and the winds whip in hot and dry from the high desert out near Victorville. Smog backs up, forming a thick layer of tan grunge along the beach horizon. Natives carp about the weather. God's mad at California.

I was doing maintenance on the *Laredo II,* a handsome cutter capable of sailing around the world. She was forty-one feet long, and I owned nine percent. Tommy and Midge Talbot owned forty-one percent, and Edward J.

Hennessy, a big spender from Irvine, had owned the other half. Two days ago, Hennessy had died of a heart attack. His widow hated all boats, this boat in particular. She gave us thirty days to buy her out. If we couldn't, she'd use the partnership agreement to force a sale.

I was down below, working the Milwaukee drill, when Midge Talbot and a lady friend came along the pontoon catwalk. Midge, Tommy's better half, was into tennis, writing, painting, committee work, real estate, golf, sailing, and community theater. Today she wore baggy Bermudas and a blousy white shirt. The young woman with her was outfitted from Banana Republic—safari shirt, safari trousers, a yellow scarf. I turned off the drill and waved at them through the porthole. Midge waved back. Her friend—a redhead with a valentine face—stared at me through designer dark glasses.

My mind was on the work, chiseling perfect slots for the new hinges, which were one-sixteenth too wide, then drilling the precise hole for the new bolts without chewing up the teak.

Since noon, I had paced myself through the August afternoon on iced cans of Bud. I took a sip, set the Bud down, and eased the spinning bit into the teak. It was hot down here, and I was dressed for the heat—Nike runners with no socks, and a pair of khaki cutoffs I had salvaged from Vietnam.

The best job of the summer had been a dusty trip in June down to Guanajuato, into the heart of Mexico. J. Benton Sturges, a blue-chip lawyer with offices in posh Newport Center, hired me to recover what was left of a $7 million real estate trust. The "trust" operated out of a bank in Laguna Niguel, south of here, but the trusting

14

losers were spread out from Santa Barbara to Dallas to New Orleans.

When I located the thieves, there was $273,000 left of the once-fat $7 million. I brought that back home, and collected my ten percent, a hard-earned $27,300. I paid off some yowling creditors. I put $5,000 into the hole behind my fridge. And I sank $10,000 into the *Laredo II* partnership. The Talbots were both sailors. Edward Hennessy, a neighbor up in Irvine, had joked about escaping to Tahiti. We'd bought the boat in mid-July, $80,000 cash ante plus $30,000 more from the bank. Tommy was a good teacher. I was slowly learning to sail. I'd only seen Hennessy a couple of times. He seemed like a nice guy.

"Heathcliff?" Midge appeared in the doorway.

I shut off the drill. "Hello, Midge."

She fanned herself. "It's an oven down here. How do you stand it?"

"Sweat purifies." I showed her my handiwork with the brass hinges.

"Heathcliff, you do love it."

"Love what?"

"You love rebuilding the universe. That's what."

Midge had been an English major in college, back in the Midwest. Her favorite books were still *Jane Eyre* and *Wuthering Heights*, and she believed that a good woman can salvage a tormented man. In *Jane Eyre*, which I have not read, the tormented man is a blind dude who needs help getting to the bathroom. In *Wuthering Heights*, which I also have not read, the guy is a loony, chased by hunting dogs, crushed by the English gentry.

"Eddie's funeral was lovely, as funerals go." Midge

15

paused. "I cried. Tommy and I thought you might turn up."

"I've seen enough funerals. They make me edgy."

"You still might have showed up. To meet Christie." Midge's eyes were worried. "I've been with her most of the afternoon. Her mind's still made up."

"Then it's good-bye boat."

"Maybe not. Tommy's talking to some of his banker cronies. We may float a loan."

I drank some beer. Ever since a bank had pulverized my construction outfit in the seventies, my credit rating had flirted with perpetual zero. When I had cash, I paid cash. When I didn't have cash, I went out and worked. This was August, my slow season. I hadn't worked since mid-July. Bills were piling up. I drank more beer.

"Who's your friend?"

Midge's face lit up. "Didn't I mention her? Sally Anne Sparling? She just moved to the area. I met her at Nick's spa. She has a lovely personality, a pretty figure, and no steady man."

"Yeah, well, she looks too stylish for my pocketbook."

"Oh, Heathcliff. All you think about is money."

"That's because I don't have much."

"Everyone has a nest egg, tucked away in a sock."

"I wish."

Midge eyed my shorts, my battered Nikes. A streak of sweat ran down her cheek. "This heat wilts me. Come on up. Meeting Sally Anne won't cost you a dime."

"It's a deal."

I set the last hinge and packed my tools in the toolbox and drank off the last swallow of warm Bud and climbed the stairs, into the California afternoon. The sun pounded down from a position halfway between the Pacific and the blue white arch of the western sky. Midge had stripped down to a yellow one-piece, its French legs cut high to show off tan thigh, a tan hipbone. She and Sally Anne sat in the bow in striped director's chairs. Sally Anne still wore her safari suit.

"Heathcliff?" Midge called.

Heathcliff is the wacko in *Wuthering Heights,* the one the dogs got.

I stowed the toolbox and walked over. Midge turned around to give me a cheerleader's rah-rah smile. The redhead turned her head, giving me a look at her profile. The move looked practiced, like a model's pose. High-heeled shoes rested beside her chair, precisely. Her feet were pale; there was a Band-Aid on the right heel. I figured her age at twenty-five.

Midge introduced us and Sally Anne said a subdued hello. Her smile was chilly. She did not hold out her hand to shake. Her face below the shades was smooth. No accent that I could pick up. I wondered what kind of work she did. Nurse? Undercover cop? Weary airline stew? Her costume was trendy, semiexpensive. The Band-Aid made her seem vulnerable.

"Nice to have you aboard," I said lamely.

"Um. Lovely boat." She was practiced at saying the right thing. "Lovely hot afternoon. Almost . . . smoldery."

Midge chatted, Sally Anne nodded at her politely, and I dipped into the ice chest for a fresh beer. Midge always brought Heineken or Beck's. I sat there, studying the sun on the water, and thought about how we build these walls, plastic walls made of tough, transparent Plexiglas. We build them and keep them polished and engrave our names on them in gold and trot them out and make believe they're us. It was hard work, building walls.

17

Something was eating at Sally Anne.

In the white beach heat, Midge gestured, twitched, crossed her tanned legs, recrossed them, smiled, laughed as she tried to get the party going. A thin film of perspiration gleamed on her neck and chest. I decided Tommy was a lucky guy, married to her. I wondered how hot it was in Texas, Baton Rouge, Key West.

The heat didn't faze Sally Anne. Sitting there, statue-still, she looked cool as a Nestea ad, untouched, unruffled.

Captain Tommy came on board about five-thirty. Midge introduced him to Sally Anne. There was a heavy moment there, Tommy smiling the big insurance-guy smile, Sally Anne motionless as a Chinese painting, when I got the feeling they knew each other. Midge, talking away, all laughter and smiles, didn't seem to notice. Sally Anne turned back to contemplate the sea, and Tommy hurried below to admire my work.

I handed him a beer. Tommy is my height, six two, only thinner through the chest and torso. His business, the Talbot Agency, has offices in Irvine, Corona del Mar, Costa Mesa, and Newport Beach. He makes speeches, plays good citizen, wants to run for City Council, then mayor of Irvine, then assemblyman. Tommy played varsity tennis at UCLA. He was ranked once. He talks sometimes about his year on the circuit. Tommy's curious about my guns. He owns a Beretta, a Smith & Wesson .38, and a Winchester Model 1866, inherited from his grandfather back in Barstow. It was his idea to bring me in with Hennessy on the *Laredo II*.

"No luck at the bank, partner."

"Well, thanks for trying."

"We've leveraged ourselves into a corner on that

Laguna Canyon real estate. Otherwise, fifty big ones wouldn't be a problem."

"Wish I could help."

"Hey, partner. Don't jeopardize the old Murdock lifestyle." Tommy grinned as he clapped me on the shoulder. "I've got Barney Ratner checking it out. Barn knows a ton of money guys."

I'd heard that name. "Ratner. He worked for Hennessy, right?"

"Right. He'll be running EJH Designs for a while. Christie's lucky to have him." Tommy sipped some beer, then took a look out the porthole. "Let's go topside."

Going up the narrow stairs, I thought again of that look that had passed between him and Sally Anne. We were back on deck, hauling canvas, when I asked him. "What do you think of Midge's friend?"

"Never trust a woman in dark glasses." Tommy handled the wheel with an expert touch. "Too much like a mask."

As we passed Bay Isle, Midge left the bow and came back to join us. Midge's smile was bright, perky, and full of push as she jabbed me in the ribs. "My chair's empty, Heathcliff. Why don't you fill it?"

"Tough act to follow, Midge."

"Oh, you men! Go on!" Midge pushed me a couple of steps toward Sally Anne. "Earn your Heineken."

I walked forward. Sally Anne had left the chair and was now sitting, feet together, on a boat cushion on the deck, peering westward through the dark glasses. The sun hovered carefully against the sky. I said hello. She said hello. I said, "Nice evening." She agreed. I asked her how long she had known Midge. "A couple of weeks," she said. I asked her what exercises she did. "Abdomen," she said. And legs and hips and arms.

She was in good shape. "Are you a TV actress?"

Flicker of a smile. "No, I'm not. But thank you."

Cooling to my task, I asked a couple more questions. Where did she work? At a decorating firm in Newport Beach. Did she like it? It paid the bills. Her mechanical answers got shorter and shorter. She didn't ask me any questions. I got the feeling she was on vacation from being whoever she was when she was on shore.

When we passed by the breakwater of West Jetty and hit the Pacific, where the waves were bigger, *Laredo II* started to buck and roll. It was almost six and we had about an hour before the breeze died. Captain Tommy instructed me about setting the sails. For five or six minutes, Midge and I were busy shuffling canvas. When we were running smooth again, heading toward Hawaii, Midge asked me how it had gone with her friend.

"I have this feeling she'd rather be someplace else."

"She has seemed a little blue today. Maybe something happened at work."

"Maybe she wants to buy Hennessy's half of the boat."

Midge nodded absently, then moved past me to take over the steering while Tommy went below to use the head.

It was cooler now, racing west. I pulled on a shirt, went forward as the *Laredo II* heeled over. "Hang on," I warned Sally Anne.

Midge stood at the wheel, legs spread for balance. She'd put on yellow driving glasses.

Tommy hadn't been gone a minute when a big boat appeared, driving at top speed, coming up on us fast. I called a warning to Midge.

20

"I see it!"

"We're in the way!" I yelled.

"It's our right of way, Heathcliff!"

"What is it?" Sally Anne was on her feet, close to the rail.

Midge cranked the wheel. The Laredo altered course and tilted suddenly. Waves slapped the hull. I had to grab a line to keep from falling as I yelled down the stairs for Tommy.

"Tommy! On deck! On the double!"

"What's up?"

"Maneuver time!"

"Lower some canvas!"

The big boat had seen us and was turning, but Midge was still overreacting, spinning the wheel. A klaxon sounded as the *Laredo II* swept past the big boat. Someone called us through the bullhorn as Tommy took the wheel to rectify Midge's maneuver. The boom swung across the stern as we started to come about. Midge's voice was sharp and high-pitched as she justified her moves with Tommy. I was on my way to the mainsail, my ear cocked for Tommy's order, when I saw Sally Anne slide overboard.

I dashed for her, but she was already gone, and I remember seeing her leaning out, clinging to the railing with one hand, holding her position on the edge of the deck as if she were thinking about jumping, weighing the odds. The dark glasses were off. Her face had a crazy look.

"Sally Anne's overboard!" I said.

"Christ!" Tommy snapped some orders at Midge.

The *Laredo* tilted again. We were still moving, and you can't stop a sailboat in the water. It's not a car. You can't

21

slam on the brakes. I thought about that as I unhooked a life preserver from a stanchion. The life preserver was tied to a ring. The rope was 150 feet long, Philippine hemp, from Ace Hardware. "Tommy!" I yelled. "Handle the rope!"

"No!" he yelled. "Wait, partner—"

But I was already gone, into the dark green waters of the Pacific.

2

Impact. Salt water burned my eyes. I fought back the fear, swam toward the life preserver, hooked it under one arm, and turned left. A wave boosted me.

The big boat was closer now than the *Laredo II*. I saw people on her deck, and someone called to me through a bullhorn. I couldn't make out what they were saying, but a man in a blazer and captain's cap pointed to my left. I waved, turned ninety degrees, and swam against the water. No sign of Sally Anne.

The water turned blue, then turquoise. The orange sun wobbled on the horizon. Then I saw her, thrashing around, maybe thirty feet ahead of me. I swam that way. She vanished. I reached the place where I'd last seen her, groped around in the water, coughed, went under, steeling my eyes against the salt water sting. I thought I saw a shape in front of me, but it turned out to be a shadow. I went back up for air, dove again. The water weighed a ton. I felt weak, muscles losing ground. I saw her when I bobbed to the surface, lungs clawing for air. Six feet away. Maybe ten.

The *Laredo* slipped farther off now and the rope tightened, jerking me away. I cursed, let go the life preserver, and lunged through the water at Sally Anne. One hand caught her safari shirt. Our faces were close together. Her eyes were wide with fear. She fought me and then coughed some more.

On board the *Laredo II*, Tommy and Midge had the sails under control, but it would be a couple of minutes before they could switch to engine power. Meanwhile, the big boat was closer.

"This way, old chap," a voice called. "Over here."

Sally Anne kept coughing, trying to shove me away. Holding her chin with one hand, I swam toward the big boat. It was huge and white, with three levels of windows and a tall wheelhouse.

I heard the slow chug of engines and thought about a movie where the propellers had chewed up a victim. Sally Anne's eyes were closed. Faces stared down from the rail. Someone threw a life preserver over. A tanned guy in swimming trunks dove off the side. On the pointed prow, I noticed the name of the boat, the *Nautilus Syndrome*.

They hauled us on board and got me a blanket. The tanned guy turned Sally Anne over and started pumping the water out. The man in the captain's cap was bending over her. He had a red face and white hair. Someone handed me a brandy. I was shivering all over and drank it down too fast. What had happened to Midge and Tommy?

The red-faced man turned to me. "I'm Dr. Hunsaker, old man. We've alerted Bony. They'll have an ambulance

24

at the dock." Bony was the local nickname for St. Boniface, the major hospital in Newport Beach.

"What about the Talbots? On board the *Laredo II*?"

"They've been contacted and they're heading in. They said to tell you they would meet you at the hospital." Hunsaker turned to a Latino in a white coat. "Get this man some more brandy, José."

José got me more brandy. Each sip brought me back, drove away the taste of brine. "How's the girl?"

"We're doing everything," Hunsaker said. "The pulse is slightly irregular. There's been some shock. In these cases, they look worse than they are. She's a very strong young woman. I'm sure she'll be fine."

The tanned man handed a black bag to Hunsaker, who got a hypo out and gave Sally Anne a shot. "For the shock," he explained.

I nodded. Hunsaker was a doctor. He knew what to do.

The *Nautilus Syndrome* was outfitted for a maharaja and his entourage—chrome and gleaming teak and expensive bedcovers. I finished the brandy and José poured me another. We were in the channel, heading for the yacht basin. Out the window, I could see the *Laredo II*, sails lashed down, trailing a quarter mile behind. Hunsaker's boat was faster.

The paramedics had a stretcher table waiting when we slid into the dock. I went with Sally Anne in the ambulance. Hunsaker would follow in his car.

On the way to the hospital, a paramedic with a red beard held a white plastic cup over Sally Anne's mouth. He phoned in, then gave her a shot and started a glucose drip.

25

"What is your name?" he asked me. "Where do you live?"

"Murdock. I live near the Newport Pier."

He studied my eyeball with a pencil flash. "What happened?"

"She fell overboard. I went after her."

"You were lucky. We lost two people a week ago, in a dusk about like this."

At the emergency entrance to the hospital, they wheeled Sally Anne away, and then a nurse with a smiling face and frizzy hair met me at the door with a wheelchair and a blanket. It felt nice to sit down. Hunsaker arrived, looking like a captain from an ad in a travel folder. He snapped orders that sounded medical. Nurses said, "Yes, doctor; right away, doctor," and scurried about. Lucky break, getting run over by a physician. I asked for a hot shower, to stop my trembling. They gave me hospital coffee. I asked for a drink, meaning alcohol. A doctor in a green coat listened to my chest, restudied my eyeballs. I asked again for a drink. They gave me a pill. Hospitals never change.

I rested in a room filled with blue bottles and white plastic tubes. By the time Midge and Tommy showed up, I'd had a quick nap. Sally Anne was out of the ER, they said, and resting on the third floor.

"You guys missed out, not seeing the *Nautilus Syndrome* up close."

"I feel awful," Midge said. "It was my fault, the whole damn thing."

"Easy, babe," Tommy said. "It could have happened to anyone."

"I got rattled. I *know* we had the right of way!"

"Sometimes you need more than right of way."

26

Midge glared at her husband. A couple of minutes passed while we went over the incident. Hunsaker came to shake hands and say good-bye. "I've left word, Mr. Murdock. VIP treatment for you and the young woman." He and Tommy exchanged business cards. He assured me he was taking care of all hospital bills. I thanked him. He gave me a business card, too. DR. JUDSON HUNSAKER, CARDIOLOGIST, SURGEON, with offices in Newport Beach.

I waited a moment after Hunsaker had left. "Did either of you guys see Sally Anne go over?"

"No," Tommy said. "I was busy."

"I didn't either," Midge said. "What's up, Heathcliff?"

"She was standing close to the edge, almost as if she was flirting with the idea of going over."

Midge walked to the phone, carrying Sally Anne's purse. "It's the right thing to do. I can feel it." She punched in a number she read from a business card.

"It's ringing."

Tommy took the phone from her. "Better let me handle this, babe."

Midge moved away reluctantly, then said to me, "Sally Anne's always talking about her boss, Kathy. I found Kathy's business card. I thought we should call, let someone know."

"What about family?" I asked.

Midge shook her head. "They're back in the Midwest somewhere. Ohio, I think. Or Indiana." She watched Tommy at the phone.

"Yes, that's right," Tommy was saying into the phone. "Yes. No. No need to call back." He hung up, looking relieved. "Message relayed, over and out."

"Who did you talk to?"

"An answering service."

"Oh, really, Thomas!"

Tommy narrowed his eyes. "It will have to do, Midge." He turned to me. "Ready to go, Matt?"

I swung my legs over the side of the bed. "Ready."

Midge eyed my bare legs sticking out from beneath the hospital gown. "You can't enter into society like that. I'll find something."

Midge left the room and Tommy followed her out. As the door swung shut, I could hear them arguing. It was eight or ten minutes before Tommy came back with a green surgical outfit for me. "Midge is downstairs, huffing."

Thinking about how nice it was to be single, I dressed in the scrub suit, then wrapped my wet shorts and shirt in a hospital towel. The Nikes were soggy with seawater. Tommy and I took the elevator down. When the door opened, there was Midge in the center of the lobby, talking to a petite blond woman in a white and gold dress. Midge waved us over. Out by the emergency entrance, I saw a Rolls-Royce Silver Shadow. Leaning against the car was a lanky black woman in a black jumpsuit with Paris shoulder pads. She had the look of an athlete—a runner or a tennis player.

The petite blonde was Mrs. Landis Mayhew, a friend of Sally Anne's boss. She had a southern accent and ice blue eyes that lit up when she heard my name.

"Murdock?" she asked. "Did you say Murdock?" She took a step closer, her look full of piercing intensity. Her eyes reminded me of my first fortune-teller in a circus on the outskirts of El Paso. As her eyeballs dug into mine, I was ten again, and jittery.

"Yes, ma'am."

"Do forgive a nosy southerner, Mr. Murdock. I have friends by that name, back home. How do you spell it?"

I spelled it for her.

"Do you have relatives in the South, by any chance?" Her voice had that southern lilt—*Gone with the Wind,* Scarlett O'Hara at the dining table, Tara.

"Most of my dad's people came from Boston. He used to talk about cousins in Tennessee and South Carolina."

"Not Georgia?"

"I dropped out of high school in Georgia."

Midge laughed.

"Mmm. Could you perhaps be related to a Cassandra Murdoc? Murdoc without the *k*?"

"No, ma'am."

"You've been a policeman, I believe?"

The hairs raised up on the back of my neck. "Once."

"And now you work with your . . . ah . . . hands?" She was smiling now, the blue eyes zapping me.

"Why, Mrs. Mayhew," Midge broke in. "You are a mind reader! Matt was in the construction business. He does lovely finish work."

Mrs. Mayhew gave me one last penetrating look before she turned to Midge, with an invitation for an at-home Sunday afternoon at her house on Balboa Peninsula. Midge looked thrilled. Tommy didn't. At that moment, a woman in white slacks and a navy blue blouse started over our way from the information booth. She moved like an island princess. She was tanned and tall, with long legs, rich brown hair, and a long Scandinavian face.

"Ah, Katherine," Mrs. Mayhew said. "Come meet the people who saved dear Sally Anne."

Kathy Kagle, Sally Anne's boss, came up to shake

hands. She was in her early thirties. Her eyes were hazel or gray green, depending on the way they caught the light. There was an empty silence when she looked at Tommy and he looked at her. Her smile went away and I decided she was shy. Her hand was warm, the fingers long and tapering. After we were introduced, she seemed to ease back into herself and stand on a raised platform in her mind while she studied me. She tilted her head back and I saw a small scar on her chin. The nose looked more Roman than Scandinavian and called attention to her cheekbones. Her brief smile revealed a gap between her two front teeth. No one is perfect, but she was gorgeous. I wanted to know her better.

"She's doing beautifully," Kathy Kagle said. "Where did it happen?"

Her voice was low, close to a whisper, with a thrilling warmth. When Midge was finished retelling the story, Mrs. Mayhew handed me a card. It had gold letters on a white field. "Sunday, at my house on the peninsula. You must come."

I looked at Kathy Kagle, who nodded imperceptibly. I planned to be there. A voice on the loudspeaker paged Dr. Firestein.

Mrs. Mayhew and Kathy Kagle walked off to the elevators. Watching Kathy move gave me pleasure. There wasn't much talk as the Talbots and I walked outdoors, past the lanky black woman leaning against the Rolls. Her eyes followed us, and I thought I detected a smirk on her narrow face.

In the parking lot, Tommy was silent. Midge was excited about the invitation for Sunday.

"I'll have to rush out tomorrow and buy a new dress. Did you boys see what she was wearing? That white and

30

gold creation cost at least four thousand dollars! She couldn't have found it around here!" Midge paused. "It had to come from Paris."

We climbed into Tommy's Volvo 760 Turbo. It was metallic blue, with leather seats. Tommy started up, then turned to Midge. "No party for me on Sunday. I've got that round-robin."

"Suit yourself, babe. I've heard about her parties. They're famous, and so are the guests. I'm going."

Silence filled the car as we headed out the twisting circular drive. Midge turned in her seat to look at me. "Wasn't that exciting, the way she read your background?"

"Sure. Made my eyes feel like tea leaves."

Tommy was driving too fast down Newport Boulevard. "She wants Matt for some dark experiments," he joked. "She'll conjure his spirit all the way to the pyramids, where he was a hit man for the pharaohs."

Midge ignored him. "Christie will die when I tell her. An invitation to Mrs. Mayhew's."

"What do you know about Mrs. Mayhew?"

"Not much," Midge said. "She arrived here four or five years ago, with lots of money. She bought three houses on the peninsula. Then she tore down two of the houses and added onto the one remaining. It's featured in the paper at least once a year."

"On the sports pages?"

"Heathcliff! Of course not."

I thought I knew the house. "Where is it?"

"On Channel, I think. Near West Jetty Park. We passed it tonight, going both ways."

I knew the house, a big three-story with an enclosed compound. It was on my jogging route. Something tugged at my mind. "How long would it take to drive from her house on Channel to Bony?"

"Fifteen minutes," Tommy said. "Maybe twenty."

"Why would you want to know that, Heathcliff?"

"Because they got there fast. Tommy talked to an answer service. I waited less than ten minutes for my new hospital greens. She was there, talking to you, when Tommy and I made the lobby."

"Maybe they were closer than that," Midge said. "Maybe they were at a posh little bar on Coast Highway."

"Maybe. How long had you been talking with her before Tommy and I got downstairs?"

"Only a few moments, Heathcliff. You're in shock, dear, from your heroic exploits in the deep. You must try to relax. Take a couple of minutes off from your profession. There's nothing sinister here . . . except money and more money." Midge let out a long sigh.

It still worried me. I had a clear memory of Mrs. Mayhew's eyes, her mind probing mine. "What do you think, Captain?"

The Volvo pulled up to the stoplight. "I think I've got a tennis date for Sunday."

"All right," Midge said huffily. "I'll go with Heathcliff."

"Are you going, Matt?"

"Sure. Why not? August is slow. Maybe I can pick up a client."

"I'm sure you can," Midge said. "I'll do some marketing for you."

Tommy said nothing, but he was still driving too fast. The Volvo rolled across the bridge to Lido Isle. If you turned left, you headed for the high-rent district of the super rich. If you turned right, you headed for the Newport Pier, where I lived.

"I wonder where she got that dress," Midge said. "I can hardly wait to tell Christie."

Tommy turned in his seat, his mouth open to say something to his wife. Then he clamped his mouth shut and turned right, away from the fabulous wealth of Lido Isle, toward Newport Pier.

3

It was almost noon on Saturday when I stopped off at St. Boniface. I handed over the green scrub suit, and the woman at the reception desk looked at me like I was a thief. I chose that moment to ask Sally Anne's room number. The receptionist, a blonde who smelled like cigarettes, made me wait while she checked her roster. It took forever.

"She's checked out."

"Checked out? When?"

"This morning."

"What time?"

She eyed me with malice. "This morning."

"How was she?"

"What kind of a hospital do you think we run here? She was discharged. They're not discharged unless things are hunky-dory. She's out. That means things are hunky-dory."

34

The receptionist had the kind of mentality that sent entire nations to war.

Perplexed, I phoned the Talbots. Maybe Midge had checked with her. Maybe she'd checked with Midge. But Midge's phone didn't answer, and while it was ringing, I remembered she was going shopping for a party dress to impress Mrs. Mayhew and her ritzy Balboa Peninsula world. Well, it was none of my business. Sally Anne was young. The young bounce back fast.

Holding that thought, I did my ritual run with the red Heavy Hands—a couple of miles north, up Newport Boulevard, through Costa Mesa, with a loop back southeast on the edge of Newport Bay, and then down picturesque Dover Drive to Pacific Coast Highway. Traffic was heavy for a Saturday. The summer smog was building, and by the time I got home, my running shirt was soaked.

I worked most of the afternoon on my house, Murdock's castle. It's the only real estate I ever owned, a two-story building at the edge of the beach near the Newport Pier. Terry's Surf Shop is downstairs. I live upstairs, with memories and a gun collection and Uncle Walt's carpentry tools and items of importance left behind by people who've drifted through my life. A hairbrush, left by Janna. A blouse, left by Mollie. A bikini top, left by a girlfriend of Webby Smith, my pal on the Laguna Beach PD. A photo, left by Meg, while she was going through R and R and rebirth.

I inherited the place from my Uncle Walt, my mother's oldest brother. He taught me carpentry, and one of my ambitions is to be half as precise with tools as he was. Uncle Walt's tools were his pride and joy. He was better with a handsaw than any machine. He could drive a five-inch nail with two easy taps of his hammer. The tools are stored neatly in the back room, which doubles as a spare bedroom and a workshop.

Today, I worked on building a section of my new entertainment center. When complete, it will stretch along the south wall to butt up against the gun cabinet. I've built cubbyholes for my ancient RCA television, my ancient stereo, my Radio Shack speakers (used, from the classifieds in the *Orange County Tribune*), and my ancient answering machine.

I knocked off at four to drink my first Bud of the day while I put together a pot of Murdock chili. In the summer, I add more cayenne to make the inner heat of the chili balance the outer heat of the world. Most people think it's too hot. You temper the heat, I explain, with cold beer. I was slicing the fifth clove of garlic and the meat and onions were sizzling happily when Midge Talbot called.

"Heathcliff, can you come right over?"

If it was a home-cooked meal, the chili could wait. "Sure. What's up?"

"We're having a drink. Christie's here." Midge paused, letting the silence build, then whispered, "You could actually save the *Laredo*!"

"Can she goose my credit rating?" I smelled a client.

"Don't joke, Heathcliff. Eddie collected gold coins. The collection's missing. Christie needs your professional help, getting it back."

"What was it worth?"

"Half a million dollars!"

The client smell was stronger. It was August, people are off on vacation, and business can be slow. "Give me thirty minutes."

36

Humming some bars from "Ragtime Cowboy Joe," I took a fast shower and dressed in my summer sleuthing clothes—Levi's with a crease, a white shirt, boots, and a fairly new Australian bush jacket from Eddie Bauer. I wear size 44, and the jacket is a 46, to hide the shoulder holster. I decided not to pack the .357, but I took the jacket along to look formal and businesslike.

The Ford pickup was in Slavick's in Costa Mesa for an engine overhaul, so I drove the Plymouth. She's a '69, V-8, metallic green, 420 horses, automatic windows, a police scanner, and a four-speaker stereo. Since OPEC let the air out of gas prices, I figured to keep her forever.

I drove inland, along Jamboree, until I came to the road leading into the Irvine hills, baked brown by the summer.

Midge and Tommy owned a home in Turtle Rock, in a secluded neighborhood on a tidy cul-de-sac in upscale Irvine. The street was named Tamarack. The house was two stories, 3,700 square feet, with a sunspace to the south, a brick walk leading to a brick porch, custom cupolas, and custom leaded-glass windows flanking the custom door. Big trees gave the place a peaceful feel.

Midge met me at the door. She wore white shorts and a striped jersey. Her bare feet and legs gave her a college-girl look. "Tommy's playing doubles," she said, "at the club. Just wait until you see my dress."

"Did you know Sally Anne had checked out?"

"Oh, sure. She phoned me from the airport. She's flying back home for a few days."

"How did she feel?"

"She felt fine. And she said to tell you thanks."

"Were you surprised?"

"Not really. She works out like a demon. She stays in

37

marvelous shape. And she really did sound fine on the phone."

So much for my suspicions. I followed Midge through the house to the family room, where Hennessy's widow sat on the sofa, at the far end, facing the French doors. Midge introduced us.

"I'm sorry about your loss, ma'am. I know it hurts."

Her eyes flicked over me, then away. "Yes. Thank you, Mr. Murdock. My husband spoke of you. You're the private detective?" She said it almost to herself.

"Yes, ma'am."

"Do sit down." She had a slight trace of accent—Texas, or perhaps Oklahoma. Mrs. Hennessy was a medium tallish lady whose face was lined with strain. She wore her blond hair in a frizzy, singles-bar style that was too young for her years. I figured her for forty-five. Her eyes were weary. The pale blue dress accented her mourning and didn't do much to hide the fact that she was thirty pounds overweight. A matching blue purse sat on the floor beside the sofa. In her left hand was a wineglass. In her right, a smoldering cigarette.

A large wedding ring winked at me as she finished her wine in a quick gulp and tried to set the glass down on the table. The cigarette got away from her. She made a futile grab for it and smashed the wine glass on the arm of the sofa. She swore under her breath, pounded the sofa helplessly, and stood up.

Life had tumbled in on Christine Hennessy.

"Oh, God, Midge. I'm sorry."

"Honey, don't worry."

I got to the cigarette before it did much damage.

Midge took the time to hug her neighbor before leaving the room. I squatted down to pick up shards of glass.

Mrs. Hennessy was coughing, breathing harshly. As Midge came back with a broom and dustpan, Mrs. Hennessy blew her nose and muttered a tense apology. "I keep running into things at home. It makes me feel hopeless . . . helpless. More than anything, I hate breaking things."

Midge patted Mrs. Hennessy's hand. "Christie," Midge said. "Matt can help."

"I just hate breaking things." She spoke, staring at the floor.

Midge went back to the kitchen to toss the glass and fetch fresh drinks. Silence bloomed in the room. I heard the fridge opening and the clink of a bottle opener. Midge reemerged, with a Beck's for me and another glass of wine for Mrs. Hennessy. Midge gave me her be-good look, then left us alone.

"Well," Mrs. Hennessy sighed. "Where should we begin?"

"Midge said some coins were missing."

"Yes. Ah . . . my husband's coin collection," she began. "It . . . this is very awkward for me."

"Where did he keep it?"

"In a safety-deposit box. Eddie was a Depression baby, you know, conservative about money. He had collected coins since before we were married. People—dealers— would consult him for opinions."

"Any idea what the collection was worth?"

"Half a million dollars, or thereabouts."

"When did you last see the coins?"

"I saw some in June, what my husband called French Roosters, a World War I vintage. He'd had them polished. He brought them home from the bank. They were very pretty."

"Which bank?"

"Barclays, in Newport Beach. We have a household account there."

Three years ago, I'd located a coin collection worth over a million. Coins have a way of disappearing, and you need to get moving before they slide through the cracks. "Would you like me to check into it?"

"I do need assistance. And Midge says you are . . . honest. And extremely straightforward." She looked at me for a long moment. "Can I assume you'll be discreet? You'll keep me informed?"

"Of course."

"What do you charge?" She lit a cigarette and blew out a puff of smoke.

"Forty an hour, plus expenses. If the job runs over seven hours, I get two fifty a day."

She didn't bat an eye at the numbers. "Very well."

"I usually collect a retainer, up front."

"Very well. My checkbook is just around the corner."

Midge came back into the room. "Well, how's it going? Case solved?"

"Mr. Murdock has agreed to help, my dear. May I use your little girl's room?"

When Mrs. Hennessy was out of earshot, Midge turned to me. "Did she tell you?"

"Sure. Half a million in gold coins. It used to be in Barclay's, in a lockbox. Now it's gone."

"Not that, Heathcliff. About the woman."

"What woman?"

"She thinks Eddie was sleeping around, cheating on her. She didn't say it quite that way, but she thinks he died in bed—someone else's. She just admitted it this afternoon, after some Chardonnay. Poor Christie, she's been holding that inside her for God knows how long."

"The paper said his body was found behind the wheel of his car, in a parking lot."

Midge's eyes gleamed. "Ron's Supermarket, three miles from here! Doesn't it make you burn with questions?"

"Like who moved him?"

Midge gave me a delighted hug. "See. You're already working. I love it!"

In my mind, I could see Edward Hennessy, the round face, the shock of reddish hair, the smiling eyes. Hennessy had weighed two twenty, at least. When someone that heavy dies in bed, you need two strong men and a stretcher to move the body.

"What do the police say?"

Before Midge could answer, we heard Mrs. Hennessy coming back.

"What are you two whispering about?" Mrs. Hennessy stood in the doorway. "Not that awful boat, I hope."

"Christie, honey. Things will work out."

"I didn't want Eddie to buy it. Now that he's gone, I want to rid my hands of it. My daughter thinks we should . . ." Mrs. Hennessy was still shaking her head as Midge walked us to the door. Outside, the August heat felt thick.

The Hennessy place was around the corner, on Orchard Circle, a big Cape Cod two-story, cream color with tan trim. It dominated the end of the cul-de-sac. The houses here were more expensive than anything on Tamarack. We were on the brick walkway, approaching the Hennessy place, when she told me her other-woman theory. "It pains me to say this, Mr. Murdock, but I suspect that . . . my husband was seeing another woman."

I didn't tell her Midge had already told me. "What makes you think that?"

"For the last year, he got into the habit of working late. He took many business trips . . . with his secretary. She is a pretty little thing, if you like the type, and you know how some men are with their secretaries." She sighed. "In addition, I find the police report lacking."

"In what way?"

She unlocked the front door and we stepped inside, into a big living room with a cathedral ceiling and windows of leaded glass. The place had a formal feel, everything was neat and tidy, the dining table could seat twenty. I followed her into the kitchen. On the kitchen table was a neat stack of real estate crib sheets. The one on top had the key numbers on a house for sale in Corona del Mar, 2,470 square feet for $882,000. In Corona del Mar, you had to pay for an ocean view.

"Would you like something? Coffee? Tea?"

I wanted another beer. "Coffee would be fine."

She busied herself at the built-in range, putting a kettle on to boil. The kettle was polished brass. She measured coffee into a white Melitta coffee maker. When we were settled at the table, she told me her scenario about how her husband had died. It wasn't complete, but it had a grieving widow's intensity.

"Eddie hated to shop, Mr. Murdock. He found it boring. On special occasions, a family barbecue, say, he would shop at El Rancho, down the hill. I cannot envision him shopping at another store. I take care of my home. Eddie takes care of business. I can't remember the last time I asked him to stop off for something after work. He

was just so busy." She sipped her coffee. "Or so it seemed."
She looked at me. "There is one other thing. It was discovered at the funeral home."

"What's that?"

"His wedding ring was not on his finger. It turned up
in his jacket pocket. We have been married over twenty
years. I have never seen him remove that ring. It was a
gift from me. He wore it, always."

"They put it back on at the funeral home?"

"Oh, yes. For the services."

"What's his secretary's name?"

"Gonzales. Dottie Gonzales."

"How big is she?"

"How big?" Mrs. Hennessy blinked at me. "Petite, I
would say. A size seven."

I made some notes in my notebook. "If he took the
coin collection out of the bank, where would he put it?"

"It's not in our safe here at home."

"Is there a safe in the office?"

"Yes. I thought of that."

"Do you have the combination?"

She sighed and looked hopeless. "Eddie kept it in his
head. He kept everything in his head."

"How soon can we get in there?"

"Into the office?"

"Yes."

"Monday, I suppose. Do you actually think—?"

"It's a place to start. Who would have the combination?"

"Dottie Gonzales." Mrs. Hennessy exhaled a large puff
of smoke. "Oh, I see where your questions are leading.
You don't think—?"

"I don't know, Mrs. Hennessy. Is your safety-deposit box in both your names?"

"Yes."

"Could you find out when your husband was there last?"

"I suppose so. Midge said you were quite thorough." She blew smoke at me. "Not a word of this to my daughter. It would kill her to think her father—"

I indicated the rest of the house with my ballpoint. "Did your husband have a study here, where he'd bring work home?"

"Oh, yes. Upstairs. Would you like to see it?"

"Just for a minute."

Mrs. Hennessy led me upstairs and left me alone. I poked through her husband's study. The desk was a jungle of papers, note cards, and books left open and face down. A Macintosh computer sat on a separate table. I flipped the switch on and the screen came to life. In the desk I found several Macintosh disks. They had labels like MONEY MARKETS, EJH FINANCE, SECURITIES, and GOLD. I put them into a soft red case with a Velcro closure and turned the Mac off. Computers are not my thing.

In the paper jungle were several printouts of a diagram, a labyrinth he'd drawn on his computer with a monster at the center. The monster was humpbacked, like a prehistoric frog, with a skinny tongue. At the end of the tongue was a triangular-shaped spade. In the right-hand corner was a question: "Where am I?"

The walls were packed with books, magazines, folders, files of newspaper clippings. The phone rang twice, then stopped. I kept probing.

One wall of bookshelves held computer magazines—

Macworld, Personal Computing, PC World, Byte, InfoWorld. Another held business books—*In Search of Excellence, Megatrends, Marketing Warfare, The Money Masters, The Seven Laws of Money, Funny Money, The Next Economy,* and several books on gold coins.

The third bookshelf held fantasy and science fiction, with one whole shelf devoted to Isaac Asimov. I flipped open a couple of paperbacks to discover that E. J. Hennessy had been a heavy annotator. He printed terse comments. "Hot damn. See p. 216, Jung archetype analogy." And then: "Space virgin, #27 anima analogue, body double, City of Desire."

On the inside covers were drawings—landscapes and creatures from fantasy planets—and I tried to put myself in Hennessy's shoes. He'd escape, come in here, lock the world out, and ease into the creative mode.

On the desk was a framed photo of the Hennessy family showing a teenage girl and two proud adults. The girl looked sixteen or seventeen. She smiled into the camera, displaying Hollywood charisma, teeth, a poochy adolescent figure.

Mr. Hennessy was younger than I remembered him, and not so heavy. He'd been a pleasant-looking man, round-faced and smiling. His reddish hair was getting thin on top. The intense blue eyes staring out were a window to his creative streak.

In the photo, a younger, thinner Mrs. Hennessy faked a smile beneath troubled eyes. The blue dress, a twin to the one today, had more cleavage. In the photo, she had a hand on her daughter's left shoulder. I guessed the photo was four or five years old.

I was studying the frog diagram again when I heard movement from the hallway, a muffled cough, Mrs. Hennessy stirring around. "Will five hundred be all right?" Mrs. Hennessy spoke from the door.

"Yes, ma'am."

She handed me the check. "Not a word of this to my daughter. She's in a special seminar, preparing for graduate work. I don't want this to . . . damage her."

I nodded. "Can you use the computer?"

"No. Eddie tried to teach me, but he was too impatient to be a teacher. The poor man."

"I'll take these disks along. They may tell us about the coin collection in detail."

The doorbell rang and Mrs. Hennessy excused herself and went to answer it. Out the window, I saw a tan sedan parked at the curb. It had the unmistakable look of a police car. I used a ruler to poke around the underside of Hennessy's desk, between the middle drawer and the top, but found nothing. I removed the bush jacket and tucked the folder containing the disks into it. Then, wondering if Dottie Gonzales had moved Hennessy's body from her bed to a supermarket parking lot, I walked downstairs.

There were two men with Mrs. Hennessy in the living room. The heavyset man was Lieutenant Ramirez, a special investigator for the California Highway Patrol. His collar was too tight and his jacket was rumpled.

The thin man with the eyes too close together was a federal cop, Special Agent Dorn, from the DEA. Dorn had a way of smiling that sent chills up my spine. The eyes were gunmetal gray and the shoes had a high polish. His blue suit, a snappy three-piece, was straight from Botany 500.

We shook hands and studied IDs. Dorn smirked when he handed mine back. "I've heard about you, Murdock."

"Hope it was all good things."

46

"We're checking in with all the local PIs. We'll be getting around to you."

"Terrific."

Mrs. Hennessy was smoking again. "These officers want to search my house, Mr. Murdock."

"Do they have a warrant?"

"We could get one," Dorn said. "We hoped we'd have some cooperation."

I turned back to Dorn. "I've been retained by Mrs. Hennessy. Mind telling us what you're looking for?"

Dorn looked at Ramirez. "We'll know when we find it."

"Want my advice, Mrs. Hennessy?"

"Yes. Of course."

"Wait until they come back with a warrant. Exercise your rights as a citizen."

"I have nothing to hide." She took a long drag on her cigarette and stared past me. "Well, all right. Officers, I am afraid I cannot allow you to—"

Dorn glared at me. "Would it be all right if we asked a couple of questions?"

"Mr. Murdock?"

"No problem."

I told Mrs. Hennessy we'd be in touch and walked out. Dorn's eyes bored into my back, glared at me. I went around the corner to my Plymouth and stowed the tapes in the trunk. I was opening the driver's door when Dorn and Ramirez pulled up beside me.

"Get in," Dorn said from the back seat.

I got in. The air conditioner hadn't had time to cool things down yet. Ramirez was smoking a cigarette. Dorn did the talking.

"Tell us what you're working on for the lady."

"Trying to recover some stolen property. The nature of

the property is confidential. What did you boys hope to find in there?"

"This is a federal case, Murdock. It goes very high up."

"So did Watergate."

"How would it be if I asked the local police to jerk your license and carry permit?"

"How would it be if I talked to a federal judge about your pushy visit to Mrs. Hennessy?"

"Pushy?" Ramirez asked.

Dorn sighed, then leaned back against the seat. "Okay. We're working a combined task force operation. The net extends from L.A. to the border, from there all the way to Houston, New Orleans, and Miami. The big money's in executive dope, and we're tracking a cocaine trail from the boardrooms of America straight to the Border Mafia." He lit a cigarette and looked at me. "You know how Edward Hennessy died?"

"Heart attack, I heard."

Ramirez spoke for the first time. "Yeah. But brought on by the white stuff."

"It interrupted the signal to his heart," Dorn said. "Hennessy was the third executive to go from coke in the last three months. The business community wants action, and they have a voice in Washington. We think this is just the tip of the iceberg in Orange County. We're tracking his supplier."

I thought about Dottie Gonzales and nodded. "Good luck."

"What we want from you is cooperation."

"I always cooperate with the law. I was a cop once myself."

"Big patriotic speech." Dorn cut his eyes to Ramirez. "So what's the job for Mrs. Hennessy?"

I opened the door of the tan sedan. "Tell you what. If I stumble onto the cocaine trail, I'll let you know."

"'Stumble' is the operative word," Dorn said.

"How about 'tripped'?" Ramirez said.

"We'll be talking to you, Murdock. And not a word to Mrs. Hennessy about the coke."

I got out and closed the door and stood there watching the tan sedan roll down Tamarack. Across the street, two kids wearing baseball gloves were winging a tennis ball back and forth. They both had good hands, but one kid had better footwork.

To make it in life, you need both—good hands, good footwork.

I drove home and made some phone calls. Dottie Gonzales's number didn't answer. I called Webby Smith, my pal on the Laguna Beach police who stays in shape at forty-three so he can handle the triathlon. Webby knew about Dorn's task force. It was called Operation Clean Sweep, and all the top-ranking police officers in Orange County were being kept guardedly informed. By Monday, Webby said, they'd have a court order to open Hennessy's office safe.

"How's the rest of the Hennessy case shaping up?"

"What do you mean?"

"Was there an autopsy?"

"There is. And there isn't."

"What's that mean?"

"They did one, but they're not making the findings public. This guy Dorn, he's big on control."

"When does the family get to know?"

"About the coke?"

"Yeah."

49

"Not for a long, long time."

"So the official reason for death is natural causes?"

"Right."

"And we know the coke killed him?"

"Contributed, right."

"And how do you feel about that?"

"Me, I got three hundred thousand tourists in my town, spread out across five weeks of summer. My town is Laguna. The guy died in Irvine, for Christ's sake. There's a heavy Fed tromping around, dressed in three-piece suits. Why should I bother?"

"What if Hennessy died lying down?"

"In his car?"

"Yeah."

Webby sighed. "Okay. Okay, I'll check into it. And you buy the next lunch. Okay?"

We made a date for one o'clock at the Ancient Mariner on Friday. I wanted to be at Hennessy's office before Agent Dorn, so I called Mrs. Hennessy to set a definite time for our Sunday morning visit to EJH Designs. The daughter answered. When Mrs. Hennessy came to the phone, her voice sounded thick with drink as she said a reluctant okay.

I cooked a steak and spent the evening watching television, thinking about Hennessy and cheating. You fall in love and get married and then love fades and that spooks you and so you get desperate looking for a replay of first love—flowers and romantic music and long, long sighs. You forget that time has passed, and instead of growing up and facing the clock, you try infidelity. At first, infidelity is exciting—stolen moments, passion, breathy sighs—but then the music dies and that turns ugly, too.

I needed to talk to Dottie Gonzales.

4

EJH Designs, Inc. was located in a green-lawned complex of gray, ultramodern industrial buildings just off the San Diego Freeway in Irvine. Leaving the beach, it was overcast, but five miles inland the day turned sunny, just right for a Sunday afternoon party on Balboa Peninsula.

I turned off on Jamboree, drove past three hotels under construction, and had to stop at the EJH gate to wait for Christine Hennessy. When she arrived, driving a cream-colored Cadillac, I left the Plymouth at the gate and rode in with her, past the guard at the guardhouse. I carried my favorite army rucksack, olive drab, with shoulder straps. In my profession, you need to have your hands free.

The entrance road curved to the right, past a small clump of trees, and then the buildings appeared ahead, black metal and dark glass. It was almost ten, and intricate watering machines sheeted the lawns with water.

Today Mrs. Hennessy looked calmer, more in control.

Instead of perpetual blue, she wore severe white slacks, a white blouse, a yellow jacket. Her blond hair was pulled back, making her cheekbones more prominent, her worried eyes more hollow.

"This was awkward for me, Mr. Murdock. I was forced to make several calls."

"I appreciate it, ma'am. And we need to get moving."

"Well, if you say so. And it was strange, not cooperating with those policemen."

"Yes, ma'am."

She parked with a jerk in the slot marked HENNESSY and we walked through the gathering heat to the main building. The sign—EJH DESIGNS, HEADQUARTERS—was in big silver letters. A uniformed guard toting a pistol and a walkie-talkie let us in. He didn't know Mrs. Hennessy, but he nodded okay when she showed him her husband's plastic ID. Inside, we were hit by a wall of cool air. Off to the right, a closed door marked AUTHORIZED PERSONNEL ONLY. Above the door, a blinking red light.

We went left, past a woman security guard sitting behind a desk, watching six closed-circuit TV monitors. She glanced at Mrs. Hennessy with no sign of emotion. "Along this corridor, turn right. His name's on the door."

"I know my way around, thank you."

When we were almost to the door, Mrs. Hennessy gave me a bleak smile. "I haven't been here since the remodeling. Eddie moved his office."

We opened Hennessy's door and walked into a reception area with a glass-topped receptionist's desk, black filing cabinets, a locked glass case displaying computer games. There were four chairs and a red sofa for people waiting to see the president. To the left, a smaller office

52

behind a glass wall. On the door was the name DOTTIE GONZALES, ASSISTANT TO THE PRESIDENT.

"This way, Mr. Murdock."

Mrs. Hennessy led me through another door, into Hennessy's office. The desk at home had been messy; the one here was L-shaped and clean. The room smelled of industrial-strength disinfectant and the iron blue carpet was spotless. A Macintosh, twin to the one at his home, sat on the left arm of the L. Mrs. Hennessy marched to the desk, sat down in the blue swivel chair with the chrome legs, and tried to open the drawers. They were locked. She got red in the face trying.

"I asked Barney to have these unlocked."

I produced my set of lock picks. "Let me give it a try."

"Very well." She opened a door leading to a dressing room and executive bath with white tile. As I focused on the middle drawer, I could hear her clicking the dial of a wall safe. She swore again. "Darnit!"

I had the drawers open in less than ten seconds. The last one opened as Mrs. Hennessy stepped out of the dressing room. "Eddie's safe. I can't do a thing with it. Perhaps we should wait on Barney."

"Is he coming?"

"He said he'd be here. I told Eddie about this, about keeping everything in his head. I warned him." Then she eyed the open drawers. "Well, Midge did say you were clever."

With the drawers open, we went to work without waiting on Barney. Mrs. Hennessy took the swivel chair. I sat on the floor. We found more computer disks, a small address book, a new leather ledger with the words "personal finance" written hurriedly across the front page, but nothing written inside.

"Lizzie gave it to her dad. Last Christmas."

It was weary work, going through the desk. Above us, the air conditioner whirred, shoving cold air into the room. We'd been working for ten minutes when Mrs. Hennessy excused herself to smoke a cigarette.

Probing with a pencil flash, I found Hennessy's private journal taped on the underside of the desktop. I pulled the middle drawer out and looked, and there it was, six inches by nine inches, with a red plastic cover. The pages were curled from much sweaty holding. The corners were dog-eared. The first twenty pages listed numbers, some with fractions, some without. They could have been stock quotations. After the fractions, Hennessy had written stabbing exclamation points. The next ten pages of the book were blank, as if Hennessy had blocked out room for later entries.

There were snatches of poems, written fast on the right hand page, and then recopied on the left in a more legible hand. In the poems, a man kept chasing after elusive women and falling on his face. It seemed like a proper subject for poetry. At least twenty of the poems had numbers for titles. "Number 12." "Number 18." "Number 6." The numbers referred to different women. What number was Dottie Gonzales?

In the middle of the book, I found a list of telephone numbers. Some were local. Some had the Los Angeles area code. On the back cover, Hennessy had written the measurements for a centerfold dream girl: 37, 23, 35. Might as well try it. I pulled on some gloves, walked into the closet, and ran the numbers on the dial of his wall safe. The tumblers clicked and I opened the safe. Well,

well. Inside, there was a clear plastic envelope containing a half ounce of white powder. I guessed it was Hennessy's cocaine stash, part of the batch that killed him. There was no coin collection in the safe. I put the envelope back, for Dorn and his court order, and then I slid Hennessy's spare suits back along the rack, in front of the safe.

I sat at Hennessy's desk while I made some phone calls. The first number reached a mechanical voice telling me the number was no longer in service. There was no new number.

The second number rang three times. A female voice answered, sexy, liquid, breathy.

"This is the answering service. How may I help you?"

"I'd like to order a pizza."

"I'm afraid you have the wrong number, sir."

"How about a massage?"

There was a pause and then the sound of keys clicking. "Could you code in, please?"

"Sure. Thirty-seven, twenty-three, thirty-five."

"We are processing. Please wait a moment."

I heard the muted beeps as the numbers were punched into a computer. There was a click while the computer beeps were replaced with junk rock, and I was on hold. I leaned back in Hennessy's chair. The voice came back on. "I'm sorry, sir, this code seems to be out of order."

I was about to argue when she hung up.

I was trying the 213 number when there was the sound of a big bike roaring to a stop, a deep-throated rumble, then the screech of brakes underneath Hennessy's window. When I looked out the window, a burly man in tennis clothes was taking the key out of the ignition of a big Kawasaki motorcycle. It was a Ninja 1000, called a "Café

Racer," with speeds up to 160 miles per hour—the kind of bike the cops don't bother to chase.

I was still standing by the window when the door opened and Mrs. Hennessy came in, followed by the guy in tennis clothes. His white tennis cap was tilted back on his head to make him Orange County's Mr. Friendly. Beneath the hat, his face was square, dark, dangerous. He had a thick torso, beefy arms, solid legs, a stiff, high-assed military walk. Naval Intelligence, I guessed, with that smirk. In his right hand, he carried a shiny black tennis bag.

"Mr. Murdock, this is Barney Ratner. Barney was Eddie's vice president for marketing."

"Barney Ratner, Murdock. Pleased to meet you." His hand was strong, probably from all that tennis, and he had the eyes of a liar—dark, almost black, very unfriendly. "Christie says you're hunting for a coin collection?"

"That's right."

"Eddie didn't say much about them to me. I thought he kept them buried in his patio up in Turtle Rock. Eddie was a Howard Ruff subscriber, and they're antsy about the proximity of hard cash."

"Barney never saw the collection, Mr. Murdock."

Was that another lie?

"But I'd like to help," Ratner said. "Anything you need, call on me."

"Thanks. I might."

I kept having the feeling he wanted to dig his finger into my eyeball.

He gestured at my rucksack. "What's in there?"

"Company secrets," I said.

Ratner grinned at me, then turned to Mrs. Hennessy.

"You should have waited for me, Christie. This is a secured area."

"I know. I realize that. But I'm getting so anxious about those coins."

"Hey. They'll turn up."

"And you did promise to leave the drawers unlocked."

"Hey, I told my girl to tell Eddie's girl. If they were locked, well . . ." Ratner shrugged. "Eddie's girl runs the show in here."

"Dottie Gonzales?" I asked.

"Yeah. How'd you know?"

"Her name was on the door outside."

"Oh, yeah. Sure."

"We think she might have the combination," Mrs. Hennessy said.

"I doubt it. But you can check tomorrow, when the work week commences."

"You wouldn't have her home phone number?" I asked.

"Me. Hey, I'm not a detail man. But my girl would. Or she could phone Personnel. Call tomorrow, around nine. They'll have had their coffee and be ready to put shoulder to the old wheel."

Ratner was too glib. I knew he was lying. I didn't know why. "All right. Thanks."

"And if you have any trouble, call my office."

"All right."

Now that he'd offered me services, he decided to make a speech about Hennessy and the business. "Eddie's death has us all on edge. It couldn't have come at a worse time. Here we are, in the middle of two big contracts. One for the DOD. The other for the air force. They're long contracts, three years, sometimes four, and we keep running out of cash when we get behind. Eddie was working on some bankers, to ease our cash flow problems." Ratner shook his head. "You should see that guy talk to bankers. Boy, do I miss Eddie."

Color Ratner earnest, I thought. His bouncy marketeer's smile tuned itself to the words, reinforcing, underlining. He took off the tennis cap, revealing an expensive executive haircut. I wondered if he used eye-sparkle drops, like the newscasters on the eleven o'clock news. Before he finished outlining the scenario at EJH Designs, in which he was emerging as the hero of the hour, as well as Best Friend of the Deceased, I saw tears in Christine Hennessy's eyes. The guy was good. "Could I speak to you alone, Christie? Just for a minute."

"I'll see you outside, Mrs. Hennessy," I said.

Ratner eyed the rucksack as I stepped into the outer office. Once the door closed, leaving them alone, I spent a couple of minutes checking out Dottie Gonzales's office. Her desk was neat. There was a photo of two older people, her parents probably, on the right-hand corner. I unlocked the drawers and poked around without finding anything.

Mrs. Hennessy came out with Ratner, looking flushed, dabbing her eyes with a handkerchief. He pumped my hand again and told me he'd like to help. He watched us from the corridor as we walked past the security guards into the morning. It was hotter, not a breath of a breeze. In the Cadillac, with the air conditioner going, Mrs. Hennessy asked me what I thought of Barney Ratner.

"Seems like a hard driver," I said.

"He was Eddie's best friend." She indicated his red and black Ninja 1000 as we drove past. "He loves toys." She dropped me outside the gate where the Plymouth was parked. I said I'd be in touch. She wanted to know right away if I found anything. I explained why she should report the missing coins.

"If they're stolen, and I bring in the thief, then we've laid groundwork."

"Dottie Gonzales," she said firmly. "Oh, I checked our insurance. The collection was insured for only a hundred thousand dollars. Eddie never kept things current."

"We'll find them."

"I hope so." She goosed her Cadillac on takeoff, making the big car slip away, toward Turtle Rock and the good, good life of Irvine.

It was baking-hot inside the Plymouth. I rolled the windows down to let the hot air out, turned the AC on high, and headed for Bongo Bodette's place.

In Costa Mesa, I stopped off at Trader Joe's to buy two six-packs of Coors for Bongo Bodette. Bongo lives just off Coast Highway in a three-room apartment above a French bakery. Two of his rooms are computer rooms. The third room is a combination kitchen-bedroom-sitting room with a king-size bed at one end and a table and three chairs near the sink and stove. Across from the sink and stove is a big-screen TV, which Bongo has jerry-wired to rip sports and first-run movies off the cable. He's developing a citizen scrambler to confuse the cable people when they try to run down their signal and make him pay up.

Bongo, a tubby fellow with an Arkansas accent, a bushy beard, and the memory of a Pentagon mainframe, attracts thin ladies who wear thick glasses and very few clothes. The lady who answered the door was named Lucy June Deegan. She had two degrees from Cal Poly, a techie hangout in Pomona. She was tanned to a deep brown and today she wore a purple bikini with yellow flowers. Lucy June has a yen to be an FBI agent. She thinks what I do is romantic. Flattering, but inaccurate.

Bongo was poised in front of an IBM AT, stroking the full beard while his mind played the computer like a grand piano. He wore a white sleeveless undershirt and purple shorts. He had wrestler's arms. When I came in, he swiveled to shake hands, grinned at the double six-pack, then swiveled back. "Hey, Sherlock Murdock. Be right with you-all." And then he was lost in the machine, the gleam of discovery bright in his eye. What he can do is impressive. I saw rows of numbers that looked like formulas, with brackets, parentheses, asterisks, dots. To me, it was Greek plus Chinese multiplied by Martian.

Beside the IBM was a Leading Edge. Across the table, I saw other brand names—Compaq, Apple IIe, Macintosh, Kaypro, Apricot, Eagle. Bongo, staring at a color monitor, pressed a few keys. The numbers scrolled down the screen. As the bottom line appeared, Bongo grunted. Lucy June whistled, hanging over his shoulder. "Whoo-eee!"

Bongo said: "Sumbitch." He tapped a key to start a printer, mounted on a box beneath the long table. When the printer began clicking, he hoisted himself out of the chair. I put his weight at two seventy, much of it brain.

"Beer, Sherlock?"

"Yo."

Bongo popped open a couple. Lucy June slid away, to return in a minute with three iced mugs. Bongo hates warm beer. Back in Arkansas, they kept iced mugs in the freezer of his favorite watering hole.

As we drank, I showed him the stuff in the rucksack

from Hennessy. He handed the disks from the Macintosh over to Lucy June, who was perched on a backless stool.

"Anythin' else?"

I handed over the phone numbers and told him what had happened.

"Shit, Sherlock. Them places, you gotta jimmy up through a air crack in the goddamn back door." He studied the numbers, finished his first beer, then swung his swivel chair around and used his computer keys to dial the 213 number. Digits clicked across the screen. There was a whirr, then a pause. A message in caps asked for a credit card number. "Shit." Bongo typed in a sixteen-digit number from memory. The capitalized message on-screen told us no go:

INSUFFICIENT CREDIT. PLEASE TRY US AGAIN.
SINCERELY, LIDO ENTERPRISES.

He drank a long swallow of beer, then motioned to me. "Gimme a goldang credit card."

I handed over my MasterCard. It had twelve days to go before expiration. So far, I had not received a replacement. Bongo typed in my number, then followed it with my name, spelling it "Murdoc," leaving off the *k*. He watched the screen as he sipped the beer. His eyes were narrowed, his nostrils flared. He said "Bullshit" as the message told us again our credit was insufficient. Bongo shook his head and signed off.

"What happened?"

"Data bank. Afore we lock on, we got to have thicker plastic."

"What were you into?"

Bongo shrugged. "Probably one of them corporate

fronts for the fucking Mafia. Place called Lido Enterprises. You know some fancy folks, Sherlock. Get me a credit card with some muscle, we'll try her again."

"How much muscle?"

"Five grand, I bet. Maybe ten."

We toasted his efforts. Across the table, Lucy June was working on the disks, humming softly, some tune from the fifties. "How come you spelled my name that way?"

"SOP, Sherlock. Spell my name 'Bodet,' one *d*, one *t*. Or Bodett, one *d*, two *t*s. Confuses the ass off them deputies, they come to collect."

Lucy June broke in. "Preliminary report. Hennessy, right?"

"Right."

"This Hennessy dude moves some bucks."

We walked around the table to join her. On the screen was a spreadsheet titled "Hennessy: Personal Holdings." Numbers were laid out in individual cells.

"How can you tell?"

Disdainful light flashed off her glasses as she gave me a look. "He's spent a hundred and eighty-five big ones since November of last year. This account is called Miscellaneous. He replaced a hundred fifty-five in June. He's got five personal credit lines . . . hmmm . . ."

"Any trace of some gold coins?"

"He bought gold in April, at three hundred forty-four dollars an ounce. Canadian Maple Leafs."

"What about a coin collection?"

Lucy June shook her head. "Nothing here. I'll keep looking."

"Whut's in it?" Bongo asked.

"How many coins would it take to make up a half million?"

"Today's dollars?" Bongo stroked his beard.

"Yes."

"Depends on how old they were. And how beat up. Knew a feller up Malibu way had seven coins worth a million three. Last June, a French Rooster, 1917 vintage, went for a hunderd twenty-five. If it was all Roosters, you'd need mebbe four thousand coins."

"Nice spread, chief, from four thousand coins to seven."

Bongo slapped me on the shoulder. "We'll find 'em, Sherlock."

"How's Tuesday morning for a preliminary?"

"How's Wednesday afternoon?"

"My client's in a hurry."

"Haw!" He slapped me on the back. "We'll bust our butts."

"Great. I appreciate it."

Lucy June went back to work and Bongo walked me to the door. "Thanks for the beer."

I handed him a slip of paper with Dottie Gonzales's phone number. "Can you get me an address on this?"

"On the house."

"What's this going to cost me?"

"For you, Sherlock, a hunderd bucks, cash money. And a case of Coors."

"Hey. Last time it was fifty."

"Shit. Seventy-five then. Guy's gotta eat."

"You got it."

"Hang in there. And scare us up a credit line with some sand, okay? We'll hit them phones again."

"I'll try."

Bongo liked to crack data banks. Maybe I could borrow

a credit card from Tommy Talbot, one with a higher ceiling.

Great ideas.

On my way home, I started at the hospital parking lot and timed the drive to Mrs. Mayhew's spectacular peninsula home. It was Sunday and the drive took twenty-seven minutes.

5

Midge Talbot was ashamed to drive out to Mrs. Mayhew's in my Plymouth, and she insisted we take her
Volvo—a Scandinavian red 760 Turbo, with leather seats
and a power sun roof. So on Sunday afternoon around
four, Midge drove over from Irvine and picked me up at
my place on the Newport Pier.

"Tommy's playing tennis," she said with a hurt look.
"We had an awful row. Why don't you drive."

She stepped out, skirt swirling, to turn over the wheel.
Her party dress was bright orange. It had short sleeves
and a daring neckline and a stylish New York look when
she moved. With the dress, she wore a white hat, white
gloves, and white heels. When she climbed in on the passenger side, the orange skirt billowed up, baring Midge's
tanned legs, and she grinned at me mischievously.

"I can't tell you how much this cost. The price was sim-
ply wicked."

"Watch out for the Sunday propositions."

"At Mrs. Mayhew's? Never."

For the occasion, I wore slacks and a sport coat, but no tie. I'd worn my share of ties in the army, and ties were my way of earmarking certain segments of the population—police detectives on the make, FBI agents, DEA investigators, doctors pronouncing death sentences, car salesmen on the make, fund-raisers, TV newsmen, judges, lawyers, corporation guys on the make. Eddie Hennessy had worn a tie the day we'd signed papers on the *Laredo II*. Now he was dead, leaving behind a trail of coke, infidelity, sad poems, and missing coins.

"What a glorious day!" Midge exclaimed. "Are you excited?"

I thought of Kathy Kagle. "Yeah." Traffic was medium as we cruised east along Balboa Boulevard, past stucco beach houses and kids in surfing clothes. As we neared the Wedge—where the peninsula widened slightly—the real estate escalated by quantum leaps and the houses took on a smug, regal, self-satisfied look.

A simple two-bedroom bungalow, no view, thirty feet across, went for a million at least. Mrs. Mayhew lived on Channel in a palazzo fortress with a view, a black iron security gate, and a doorman in a white tux with tails. In an area where beach frontage was worth ten times its weight in gold, her Mediterranean-style house sprawled across three choice lots.

I parked down the street. The snazzy Volvo looked small-time in amongst the Jags and Alfa Romeos.

"I was out here for a Christmas gala," Midge said as she got out. "They sure know how to party."

Up close, Mrs. Mayhew's gate guard had a thin dancer's face and a semipunk crewcut. He checked our names off engraved cards in a silver box, smiled through television teeth, and waved us inside.

"My God." Midge took my arm and stared at the lavish courtyard. The statues looked like the real thing, straight from Italy. The shrubs were bonsai trim. In the center was a marble fountain that was almost too massive for the courtyard. Three couples strolled by. The women were Newport Beach slinky, slender as snakes, and beautiful. Midge identified the men. "Well, one mayor. One councilman. And Joel Mandrake."

"Who's Joel Mandrake?"

"Only the hottest rock star going. Don't tell me you don't know him!"

"Afraid not."

"Heathcliff, you've got to get out more."

A waiter in a red jacket and blue pants with a Zouave stripe hurried across from another door carrying a tray covered with a white napkin. I could hear the sexy tinkle of female laughter as Midge and I crossed the courtyard. A big bougainvillea spilled orange blossoms in the faint afternoon breeze. Midge laughed. "Would you believe that matches my dress!" Behind a screen of bushes, I heard a man talking to a woman. The topic was not sex, but securities.

The French doors stood open, to provide access between house and courtyard. Mrs. Mayhew saw us when we came in. She stood at the other end of the room, talking to a heavyset white-haired man with a red face. It was Dr. Hunsaker, in his tennis whites. Mrs. Mayhew wore a dress of white and gold. The gold highlighted her hair.

"Another four grand?" I asked Midge.

"Five," Midge whispered back. She quickly identified

more celebrities—two state assemblymen from Sacramento; Harry McGee, the CEO for Grosspointe Industries; Warren Jones, the president of Traine Company, which owned most of the land in Orange County. I saw a signal pass between Mrs. Mayhew and her black chauffeur, who threaded her way through the snazzy crowd to escort us over to Mrs. Mayhew. Everyone was dressed snazzily, and I almost wished I'd worn a tie.

The chauffeur wore a sheer white blouse, white harem pantaloons, and silver sandals. The blouse was cut in a daring V and kept drifting open, displaying perky breasts. On her left wrist were three silver bracelets.

"Welcome to Mayhew Castle, people. I'm Latrice." Her voice was husky, with a mocking tone heightened by her sultry Jamaican accent. I smelled perfume. "This way to the lady of the peninsula."

Going through the crowd, we brushed past toothy socialites and heavy hitters busy buying and selling. "It's the Social Register!" Midge exulted. "Everyone is here!"

I recognized Mort Elwell, an ex-client from four years back. Mort was a millionaire pal of J. Benton Sturges, a lawyer who's gotten me cases in the past. As we neared Mrs. Mayhew, Latrice Paramount stopped to let us go forward and Hunsaker came forth to shake hands. I felt like a baton in a relay race.

"Well, well, old man. Good to see you." Hunsaker's smile seemed forced. "Been swimming lately?"

Party talk eludes me and I had no clever comeback. Mrs. Mayhew was crowing about Midge's dress and what it did for her coloring. I looked around for Kathy Kagle, my reason for coming, but didn't see her.

Hunsaker and I chatted for a while, and then he introduced me to three people who looked super rich and a woman in her fifties who looked super rich and predatory. I thought about my trip from St. Boniface to Mrs. Mayhew's and I turned to Hunsaker.

"You made that call, didn't you, doc?"

"How's that, old chap?" His blue eyes studied me like I was a heart patient about to be wheeled into surgery. "Which call?"

"You phoned Mrs. Mayhew on Friday. To tell her about Sally Anne."

Hunsaker's smile was intense enough to start a prairie fire. "Tell her about who?"

"The young lady who fell off the Talbots' boat. Sally Anne."

His smile stayed exactly the same. "Really, old man. I never saw that young woman before that evening. Why should I do that?"

"I haven't got that part worked out yet."

"Well, when you do, be certain to keep me informed."

And just then, Mrs. Mayhew slid up beside me, her eyes bright with promise, to take my arm with a grip I couldn't ignore. The dress dipped open at exactly the right moment, giving a quick glimpse of bronzed breasts. With a bleak look at Mrs. Mayhew, Hunsaker walked off. I'd jabbed him where it hurt, but I didn't know why. It was probably nothing.

"Mr. Murdock, let me show you my home." Mrs. Mayhew leaned into me like she was fifteen again and I was the captain of the football team. She steered me to the edge of the crowd. I was glad to be out of there. The Sunday smiles made my face hurt.

"What were you speaking to Judson Hunsaker about?"

"Sally Anne."

"Who?" Her face was total innocence.

"The girl who works for Kathy. The one who fell overboard Friday."

"Oh, yes. What a pretty child. How is she?"

"She's terrific. She's so terrific she left town."

"Really?" Mrs. Mayhew studied my face. "Yet you seem so concerned. Was there some . . . did you know her well?"

"We'd just met. Did you?"

"Did I know her? Only to speak to. She works for Katherine. Why do you ask?"

"Because of the way you hustled over there Friday night."

"'Hustled'?" Her smile was cold.

"You got there pretty fast after we called."

"Did we?"

"Yeah."

Mrs. Mayhew aimed me down a corridor with a floor made of Italian marble. "I hardly notice the time, but my Latrice does happen to be a superior driver. One might say she has her way with time and space. In here, Mr. Murdock." She opened a double door of inlaid rosewood, and we were in a library packed with books. I saw sections on diet, self-help, fashion, sexual behavior, occultism, mythology. Three shelves were devoted to the collected writings of Carl Jung. I remembered Jung's name from one of Hennessy's books.

The ceiling was twenty feet high to give room for the mezzanine level, which could be reached by a ladder on wheels. There were two rosewood desks for reading, with those little green shades you see in movies. In one corner was a portable computer. "I had no chance to attend college," she said, "so I make sure that I keep myself educated." Mrs. Mayhew strolled to the window to look out at

70

the harbor. Directly in front of the window was a private beach where people lay in deck chairs taking the sun. Just west of the beach, I could see the green windscreens of a private tennis court.

Mrs. Mayhew stood there a moment before turning back to me, making the skirt swirl around her legs. "You are a Taurus, I believe."

"How did you know?"

"Intuition. Your father wore a uniform. Soldier? Policeman?"

"Soldier." I was enjoying our little waltz, but the hairs were standing up on the back of my neck.

"And your mother. She was not Irish, but from northern Europe, Germany, I should say, close to Hamburg."

"Her grandparents came from Kiel."

"You're smiling. Why?"

"You do dossiers on all your Sunday guests?"

"This is not from a dossier, Mr. Murdock. I detect your mother in your eyes, in your hands. You are a craftsman, but your father was not. A skill like that had to come from your mother's side. An uncle, perhaps?"

Uncle Walt, I thought. "He taught me carpentry."

"Mrs. Talbot mentioned you were a builder. And your presence, the way you hold yourself, says you were a soldier."

"I was career army, until 1968."

"Soldiers detest standard uniforms," she went on. "Yet the uniform lingers in the spirit, if only for its simplicity. A uniform—such as the one you're wearing today—frees the mind for more serious work. I find dress one of the better distinctions between male and female. Birds, of course, have male plumage." Mrs. Mayhew perched on the edge of a desk, then switched subjects. "Mr. Murdock, how would you like to work for me?"

"Doing what?"

"Investigations. Security. Your forte. I have many interests. I travel quite a bit. My life has been threatened."

"Recently?"

"Recently enough for me. This probably sounds melodramatic, but I have made some formidable enemies."

I heard it, but I didn't buy it. People like Mrs. Mayhew never say what they mean or mean what they say. Trying to decode the message makes me testy. "Is there a room for me over the stable? With a hot plate and a small refrigerator? Or do I get a ration of bread and water?"

She laughed, a hearty sound for a woman so petite, and I wondered how many men she'd suckered down through the years with the laugh and the astrology and the trim ankle swinging slowly, rhythmically, like a golden pendulum. "Ah, the independent male. There are certain fringe benefits, bread and water notwithstanding. Money breeds money, as my teacher used to say. And money mixes with money, but not with anything else. Not blood. Not love. Certainly not friendship. My teacher had some marvelous sayings. I could pay you three thousand dollars a week. You could expect three weeks off a year, on salary, of course. What do you charge? Three hundred dollars a day? Two hundred fifty?"

I nodded while I multiplied three thousand times fifty-two weeks.

"Yours is sporadic work, I believe. A spurt here. A spurt there." That smile again.

"Gives me time off. Early retirement."

"Retirement is for drones."

"I'm working now. Already got a client."

"Of course." Her face clouded. "Well, when you finish that up, then."

People like Mrs. Mayhew buy and sell everything. I wondered what she wanted from me. "If I worked for you, could you teach me astrology?"

"More than that." She eased off the desk. "Come. Let me show you the rest of the house."

The house was built in a U around a central patio. We rode up to the third floor in an elevator that whispered. When we stepped out, she took my arm. "How old do you think I am?"

"Thirty-eight," I said, giving her a decade.

"Do not joke about history. I am fifty-seven years old."

I turned to look at her, the clear skin, the steady burning eyes, the pulsing energy. Put her on a TV spot, mother and daughter jogging, riding bikes, staying young forever, and sell face cream or cereal by the zillions. She looked fortyish. Fifty-seven was pure sorcery.

"I was born in the first year of the Depression. You are staring at me."

"I'm impressed."

"My secret," she whispered fiercely, "could be your secret."

We came through an extra wide door onto the roof, where she had built a sun room. Next to the sun room was a greenhouse packed with exotic flowers. There was a six-foot wall beyond the greenhouse.

We left the roof and dropped down to the second floor. The east wing was bedrooms, a recreation room with a pool table, an indoor sauna, a computer room, a library. The west wing was social—big kitchen, laundry room, dining room, the huge living room, a TV room. With the courtyard format, you could have natural light in every room. The house was decorated in her royal colors, white and gold, emblem of the House of Mayhew.

"Well, what do you think?"

"Seven million on the market. To build it today, ten."

We took the stairs down, I did the multiplication again, three thousand times fifty-two weeks.

"You are thinking about my offer, aren't you?"

"Would I furnish my own white tux?"

Her laugh was hearty. We came into the party room, where I thought I detected the smell of marijuana. If they were smoking here, it had to be the best. "And there's Katherine," Mrs. Mayhew said, pointing, and I spotted Kathy Kagle, looking beautiful in blue, in the center of the room. "Do run along now, Mr. Murdock. And do think about my offer."

Mrs. Mayhew deftly steered me toward Kathy, who was listening to a big blond man with a mustache. He wore a white Palm Beach suit, an orange shirt a shade darker than Midge's dress, and a yellow ascot. His face was billboard handsome, billboard square. He swayed to the music, but just behind the beat. I walked over to Kathy. She saw me coming and smiled. The big man saw me and frowned, and I got the impression he had the hots for Kathy. She introduced the big blond man as Landis Mayhew. His handshake would have crushed rock. He looked healthy, fit, and I figured him for a stockbroker, a preacher, or a jock.

"Mr. Mayhew was a professional tennis player," Kathy explained. "He won the French tournament in nineteen seventy-five."

"Nineteen seventy-six, Katherine," Mayhew said. "Murdock. Murdock. Ah, yes. You're the brave Tarzan who saved Kathy's little shop minion from a watery grave." Landis Mayhew had a surly manner, a surly voice. I figured him for a spoiled rich kid, born in the South. He was at least ten years younger than his wife. I wondered why Mrs. Mayhew hadn't told me he was her husband. More clever games?

"Got lucky."

"Ah, the reluctant hero. That role does have its appeal, doesn't it, my dear? I was once a reluctant hero, but that was in my heyday on the circuit." His voice was too loud.

"Mr. Mayhew," Kathy said. "Please?"

Landis took a long time turning away from her, like a big radar scanner on a naval vessel. His breath stank of alcohol. He poked me with a finger. "Who are you, sir? And why are you here, darkening my door?"

"You're drunk, buddy."

"Drunk? *Moi*? Inebriated, my mother used to say. *Moi*? Inebriated?"

Kathy looked stricken. People were staring at us with little smiles and I was running through my checklist of where to hit him without breaking anything or making him bleed when there was a ruckus over by the door and a man wearing cowboy clothes bulled his way inside, followed by the red-faced doorman in the white tux.

"Oh, God," Kathy said.

The cowboy was unpleasant-looking, an ex-jock going to fat but still capable of doing damage. He wore a western shirt with pearl buttons, Levi's with a wide belt, a Stetson, red boots, a western jacket made of whipcord twill, and a string tie. His face was meaty, his eyes beady and too close together. I figured his weight at two twenty.

"What's this?" Landis Mayhew started for the cowboy, but was waylaid by a society woman in a see-through blouse. Kathy left me and was walking toward the cowboy. Across the room, Mrs. Mayhew caught my eye and mouthed the word "Help." Kathy had reached the cowboy and led him outside. Landis broke free and followed her, stumbling, bumping into people. I followed Landis.

On the veranda, Landis grabbed my arm and shoved his face close. "You stay out of this, hero. I can handle this slime." His foot slipped getting off the low veranda and he barely caught himself before he fell. Kathy and the cowboy were deep in conversation near the fountain. Her back was toward me, but I could tell she was agitated. Landis arrived and made a grab for the cowboy. The cowboy grinned, grabbed his right arm, and slung Landis into the fountain.

Landis sat cooling his butt in the pool, cursing the cowboy. When he tried to climb out, he slipped and fell. No one came to help. Kathy took a swing at the cowboy, but he caught her wrist in one hand and bent her arm back. She saw me coming and her eyes got wide and then the cowboy let her go and turned to me, hands up in a classic boxing position. "Who are you? The U.S. Cavalry?" Then he spoke over his shoulder to Kathy. "You got 'em circling you like bees on a honeycomb, sweets." His smile was erratic. "You got 'em buzzing around. They just can't stay away."

He lowered his left shoulder, shuffled forward a couple of steps, and swung. I was ready for him, and I danced away, feeling his punch swirl the air, and then he hit me twice in the body with his left. I was up against a semipro at least. I snapped a left at his eye, then faked a right at his jaw, then two lefts, quick, on his nose. Blood spurted. One of the tests is to see if your opponent can go on once he bleeds a little. He could.

The cowboy wasn't a bad fighter. He was overweight,

but he had ten years on me. A crowd piled up on the veranda. A man said, "Kill him!" A woman said, "Call the police!" Another woman said, "No, not yet." We traded punches, searched for openings. My right eye was burning. He kept talking about Kathy in a snarling manner, and that made me angry. I popped him another one on the nose, and then followed that with a hard right to the belly. He sagged a little, but kept on fighting.

"You're not bad. For an old fart."

"Thanks. You're not bad for a fat man."

He snarled, made a bad rush, and I hit him two more times. He went to his knees. Before he got up, there was the sound of sirens over Mrs. Mayhew's wall, and the cowboy grinned at me, and then at Kathy. A long shock of hair had fallen down, covering one eye.

"Watch your ass, old man."

The police sirens were closer now as the cowboy left us. Landis had disappeared. Mrs. Mayhew was shooing the crowd back indoors. Midge came up, and she and Kathy led me inside, to a downstairs bathroom decorated in white and gold. While they were dabbing at my face with cold washcloths, Mrs. Mayhew came by with a bowl of ice.

"Who was that person, Katherine?"

"I'm really sorry," Kathy said. "We met in a bar in May and he's been following me around. I had no idea he'd—"

"It did liven up the afternoon," Mrs. Mayhew said as she handed over the bowl of ice. Poor Landis rebruised his ego, but it did give Mr. Murdock the opportunity to put on a heroic display." She smiled at me, eyes shining. "And you were brilliant."

I had the feeling I was being had.

She turned to Midge. "Mrs. Talbot, I have the strong

sense you appreciate old things. I have a modest collection of Rosenthal china. Would you care to see it?"

"Oh, yes. I would, thank you."

"Several of the pieces have been in my family for generations."

The two women walked away, leaving me alone with Kathy Kagle. "Thank you for helping. I hate it when someone . . ."

The ice felt good on my face. "Who is this guy?"

Kathy sighed. "His name is Jancey Sheridan. He has a foul mouth. He's Little Rock's gift to Southern California."

"What's his work, strong-arming senior citizens?"

"I don't know. He drives a new Camaro and always has money. When we first met, I thought he was a criminal. I still do."

"Car thief?"

She smiled. "Something sly, I should think. Something semiclever and nasty and small. He makes my skin crawl."

"I had the feeling Landis knew him."

"Oh? Why?"

Kathy was bending over me. We were close enough for a kiss, and I wondered how many guys had fought over Kathy Kagle down through the years. Right now she was having a powerful effect on me.

"He called him slime."

"Landis calls everyone slime."

We went back to the party.

Landis Mayhew had changed into dry clothes—a Banana Republic safari suit with a yellow ascot—and was seated at the piano, playing memory music from the forties. Midge Talbot stood with Hunsaker and Mort Elwell

78

and half a dozen others in a half circle around Landis as they sang along.

I had one for the road with Kathy. She didn't say much, but I still had the feeling we were communicating. I asked her for a drink Monday and she accepted. Casere's, five-thirty.

I was about to ask Kathy about Sally Anne when Midge came up, bubbling over Mrs. Mayhew's china and crystal. "Heathcliff, you wouldn't believe it! Two whole rooms!"

Kathy nodded. "It's a little ominous to eat here. You're afraid of breaking something."

"Seventy-eight place settings!" Midge said. "It's worth a fortune! 'Modest,' she called it."

We said good-bye and left the party. The sun was lower in the west as Midge and I drove back along Balboa to my place. My right eye throbbed.

"What a party," Midge said. "Thomas will be sorry he missed all those potential clients." Midge paused for some sunburned beachgoers. "I saw her lead you away. What happened?"

"She offered me a career with the House of Mayhew."

"A job?"

"More like the civil service. Sick leave, retirement benefits, vacation pay."

"Lots of money, I bet."

"More than I ever dreamed of."

Midge eased the car forward as she changed the subject. "Lord, I covet that house. If it was mine, I'd make some changes, get rid of that awful white on gold. She told me your new friend was the decorator." Midge paused. "If it helps, I like her, even if she is too beautiful.

She seems . . . simpatico. You need that, Heathcliff. You've been alone too long."

"I didn't know it showed."

"I'm a female, dear. And we females know things." Midge made a left turn off Balboa to my place near the pier and double-parked. "Did you tell her I was a Gemini?"

"Who?"

"Mrs. Mayhew."

"Didn't know you were."

"You were there, at my birthday party. Remember? It was June tenth?"

"I remember drinking a lot of beer and eating too many hot dogs. Are you a Gemini?" I opened the door and climbed out.

"I wonder how she knew?" Midge mused.

"Probably read some tea leaves."

"She's asked Tommy and me for dinner. A party, she said, in two weeks. This could be the start of something big."

"Maybe I'll be waiting tables, wearing a white tux."

"Oh, Heathcliff. You're always joking."

Midge thanked me for the escort service, and I closed the door and watched her drive off, toward Irvine, and then I went upstairs to study my battered face in the bathroom mirror. Could I have taken the cowboy? Or was I getting too old?

6

Dottie Gonzales lived in Woodbridge, a planned "village" in the ultraplanned community of Irvine. The address I'd gotten from Bongo said 7 Whistling Lane. It was a two-story condo overlooking the man-made lake about four blocks from Ron's supermarket, where Hennessy's body had been found. Everyone works in Irvine, to pay for the mortgage, the two cars, the good life. The bumper stickers read ANOTHER DAY IN PARADISE. On the lake, the ducks wheel together in majestic splendor, like rival armadas on fleet parade. There was no one around Monday morning when I parked the Plymouth around the corner and strolled up Whistling Lane and rang the bell. No answer. I slipped on my thief gloves, picked her lock, and got inside.

Condos are getting smaller.

In the main room, mirrors along the whole wall made you think you were in a bigger place. The breakfast room was sunny and tiny, with white and blue chairs, a narrow table. There were dishes in the sink, and the Kitchen Aid dishwasher was half full, with the faint smell of mold. In the fridge, something had spoiled, filling the compartment with the odor of vegetable death. I took a quick glimpse and closed the door. Three cartons of Yoplait yogurt, two cartons of cottage cheese, a half-empty bottle of Chardonnay. In the back, there was something dark green and oozing in a plastic sack.

The TV was new, a twenty-seven inch JVC with remote control and a fourteen-day video cassette deck. Above the TV sat a hot stereo system. She had a big record collection, augmented by a couple of hundred compact disks.

Upstairs, in the main bedroom, the bed was made with a pink flowered spread. The closet was packed with snappy clothes. On the dresser, there were photos of Dottie Gonzales—the same girl from the office at EJH Designs—posing with three different men. None of the men was Eddie Hennessy. The bed looked virginal, almost unused, and I had trouble picturing Hennessy on those sheets.

In the top drawer of the bedside table, I found a notepad. On the second page was the 37-23-35 combination that had opened Hennessy's safe, along with two phone numbers. One had a 213 area code and was followed by the name "Raul." The other had no area code and was followed by "El Señor R." I tore the page out and replaced the notebook. In the second drawer, I found a thin line of white powder. I took off one glove, wet my finger, tasted it.

White lady.

Dottie Gonzales was a coke-head.

I put the glove back on and walked back downstairs to search the kitchen. Hennessy's gold coins were not in the freezer, with the frozen chicken breasts and the TV dinners. They were not in the kitchen cupboards. I was just starting to search the record cabinet in the living room when I saw the unmarked tan sedan park out front. Agent Dorn got out of the passenger side, looked around like he was a cop, then buttoned his suit coat and headed up the front walk. Detective Ramirez followed.

I made sure the front door was locked before leaving the back way, onto a small patio where the plants needed watering. The fence was five feet high. There was no gate. I tore my shirt on some bushes as I climbed over. It took me a half minute to jog to the Plymouth.

I hadn't found the coins, but it was a good guess Dottie Gonzales had supplied Hennessy's executive coke. It was a good enough reason for her to run.

Before climbing the hill to Turtle Rock, I called Webby Smith in Laguna.

"Shamus," he said, "this is Monday morning. Yesterday we had fifty-seven thousand people in my city. I am irritated and depressed about my work. What is it?"

"Just checking in on Operation Clean Sweep. What's the latest?"

"They hit the Hennessy plant with the court order. Since I'm not one of the federal higher-ups, I can only assume what they found."

"Do I hear envy and professional jealousy?"

"Goddamn right. Was there anything else?"

"Any more on the Hennessy autopsy?"

"I checked. The blood was in his legs and rear end. He died sitting up."

"Someone could have sat him up quick."

"You really stretch it, don't you?"

"I'm a creative fellow."

"In my business, we call it making it up as you go along."

"Who's the county coroner these days?"

"Young guy named Hunsaker."

"Oh? How long's he been in?"

"A year or so. You know him?"

"What's his first name?"

"Hell, I don't know. George Washington Hunsaker. Why?"

"A doctor named Hunsaker ran over my boat Friday night."

"I warned you about that goddamn boat," Webby said, and hung up.

On Orchard Circle in Turtle Rock, Hennessy's garage door was up and there was a brown Porsche next to Mrs. Hennessy's Cadillac. Mrs. Hennessy answered the door in her gardening clothes, pale green slacks and a matching shirt, augmented by leather tennis shoes with a fresh coat of white. Sweat had plastered some blond hairs to her forehead. She had streaks of dirt on one wrist. Over iced tea in the Hennessy kitchen, I gave her Bongo's preliminary on her finances. She nodded, then told me Barney Ratner had confirmed that same information—approximately $180,000, spent since November, then replaced over the summer. If Barney confirmed, she wasn't worried. I told her Dottie Gonzales wasn't home.

She lit a cigarette and looked away. "I'm certain she's in on this somehow."

I decided not to tell her about the cocaine. "Mrs. Hennessy, I need to backtrack your husband's movements, those last couple of days before he died."

"If it will help."

"Have you had a chance to call the bank?"

"Of course." She blew smoke past me. "Eddie signed himself into the safety-deposit box last Wednesday."

"What time?"

"He was there when they opened."

"So he could have taken the coins out then?"

"I suppose." She stood up. "Wait just a moment." She left the table. When she came back, she carried a leather-bound notebook. "Eddie's car log. He was audited two years in a row by the IRS, so he had to record his mileage." She sat down again and opened the book. "What would you like to know?"

"What did he do last Monday? What did he do Tuesday?"

The phone rang as she was flipping pages. She handed me the book and got up to answer. "Oh! Hello. How are you? . . ."

I found last Monday. Lunch with Malcolm Friedberg. Meetings with Walter Bascom, three in the afternoon, at Bascom's office. An SBEN meeting from six to seven. Tuesday, lunch with Ratner and three Japanese guys. Wednesday, there were meetings until noon, then a meeting starting at two and lasting all afternoon. The names were Lenglen, Connolly, and Tilden. At the top of the Thursday page was a note about his daughter's upcoming birthday. "Lizzie's 22nd. Buy present."

Christine Hennessy got off the phone, poured us more tea, and lit another cigarette.

"What's the SBEN, Mrs. Hennessy?"

"Oh, that's the South Bay Executive Network. Barney and Eddie are charter members. It began as a support group for executives who owned their own company. The men get together once a week and brainstorm. Eddie

85

called it his skull session. He was awfully faithful about attending."

"Where did they meet?"

"They rented a suite at one of the hotels on Coast Highway. Barney would know exactly. So would Tommy Talbot."

I nodded, made a note. The hidden world of the corporate exec. I'd known Tommy a couple of years. We owned a boat together. But I hadn't known about the SBEN. I did know three private cops. Maybe we could form PETS—Private Eyes Therapy Society.

Mrs. Hennessy walked me to the door. While we were saying good-bye, the daughter drove up in a yellow Toyota. She parked in the driveway like she lived there and got out. The daughter had her mother's face, only younger, and an identical rag-mop hairdo. Mrs. Hennessy introduced us. She had her father's creative eyes and her mother's phony smile.

I said good-bye and drove back to the beach. A quick check with my favorite reference librarian told me Hennessy had spent Wednesday afternoon playing mixed doubles with the ghosts of three dead tennis players—Suzanne Lenglen, "Little Mo" Connolly, and "Big Bill" Tilden.

Interesting guy, Hennessy.

I spent the afternoon with Hennessy's car log. I made eight calls to my reference librarian. The pattern emerged after the fifth call and the third Bud. On the sixth call, she got testy. I kept making notes. On Monday, Hennessy would attend a meeting of the SBEN, his executive think tank. On the next Wednesday, he'd play tennis with the ghost of a famous tennis player—Connolly, Lenglen, Tilden, Brookes, Hotchkiss, Doherty,

Vines, Wilding. There were no scores reported. The guy he played the most was a German ace named Gottfried von Cramm, who'd been beaten by American Don Budge in the summer of 1937 in Davis Cup play at Wimbledon. The librarian said von Cramm had died in the war. Since January, Hennessy had played von Cramm eleven times.

In April, Hennessy had gone for a medical checkup with a doctor named "Doc H." He'd seen Doc H again in May and June, but not in July.

At four-thirty, I knocked off to shower and dress in clean jeans, a soft white shirt, and my private-eye bush jacket. At five, I was at the bar in Casere's, watching a bartender with Conan biceps draw my draft beer. At three minutes after five, the door opened and Kathy Kagle stood silhouetted against the rectangle of harsh afternoon light. She paused, hovered almost, before coming inside. She wore a dark blue suit and a blue oxford cloth shirt with a red tie. She carried a briefcase and her eyes were full of her business day. She was taller than I remembered. Watching her float through a room, any room, was beginning to nudge all other pleasures to the side.

We shook hands and sat down, and when the skirt opened, showing a flash of leg, she pulled it closed deftly. She ordered a martini, a double, on the rocks. When it came, she drank a big sip. All around us, men were watching her and envying me. It was a good feeling.

"You look illegal."

"Thank you, sir."

"Any more trouble with the Arkansas cowboy?"

"No. He's probably on his way back to Little Rock. How's your face?"

"Battered." As a matter of fact, it was hurting.

She reached into her purse and came up with a small bottle of crystals. "You know homeopathy?"

"Sounds like something for the police."

"Homeopathy is an ancient healing art." She poured a few crystals into my hand. "Let them dissolve under your tongue."

"Can I still walk out of here? Or will we need the paramedics?"

"Trust me, Murdock."

I let the crystals dissolve, and a couple of minutes later my face felt better. Amazing. "What is that stuff?"

"*Arnica montana.* It was discovered in Switzerland by grazing sheep."

"Come on."

"No. The hills in Switzerland go straight up. When a sheep would fall, he would munch on *Arnica montana.* One nibble and he was healed."

I laughed. "For a minute there, I thought you were going to read my stars, à la Mrs. Mayhew."

"Oh, that's her favorite act."

"How does she do it?"

Kathy shrugged. "It's just one of her secrets. She's into occultism and the Tarot. I've watched her at dinner parties. She'll take a perfect stranger and spell out a complete profile."

"It was spooky, having her do that."

"I agree." Kathy touched her glass to mine.

"Did she read your stars?"

"Yes. The first time we met."

"Where was that?"

"Los Angeles." Kathy put her hand on my arm and changed the subject. "Can you sail that boat? What's its name?"

88

"The *Laredo II*. And the answer is no."

"Too bad."

"But I happen to know where I can borrow a power-boat."

"It's too much trouble. It was just a whim."

But I could tell she wanted out of the bar, so I paid the check and we drove in two cars to Bay Avenue. I had expected Kathy to drive a sexy foreign car and was surprised when she unlocked the doors of a green Buick station wagon at least three years old. The rear of the wagon was full of drawings and drapery samples. Kathy changed clothes on board the *Laredo II* while I borrowed a boat from Charley Hanrahan, who runs Charley's Tackle Store.

She was waiting for me on shore, dressed in white shorts and tennis shoes without socks and a blue shirt knotted at the waist. Two young guys without shirts whistled at her as she stepped down into Charley's boat. "Hey, legs!" one called.

When we reached the middle of the bay, I asked about Sally Anne. Kathy seemed eager to talk.

"She's wonderful with people. And she adores going to lunch with customers."

"And you don't?"

"Affirmative. I hate meetings, all the corporate fakery, the small talk. And the men come on so strong."

"How does Sally Anne handle that?"

"Plays dumb. Uses her little-girl routine. It's working. We had record sales last year, mostly because of her effort."

"She seems young to be such a pro."

"She's a natural."

"I called the hospital Saturday. She'd already checked out."

"That was thoughtful of you."

"Saving single life produce instant cosmic responsibility. Old karate proverb."

Kathy smiled and stretched her tanned legs. "She phoned me from the airport on Saturday to ask for some time off. It was sudden, but Sally Anne's like that."

"Moody?"

"Impetuous. She's only twenty-five."

"How's her mood been the last few days?"

"A little odd, I guess. Why do you ask?"

"Because I think she jumped. When people jump overboard, there's a reason."

Kathy looked shocked. "Are you sure?"

"She'd pulled off her dark glasses just before she went over. Her face looked determined."

Kathy laced her fingers around one brown knee. "Now that I think about it, she's been a little blue. Of course, she's up and down anyway. In the hospital she was absolutely depressed, but I still can't see her jumping. That would be . . . suicide."

"Yeah."

"Not Sally Anne."

"You know much about her private life?"

"Not too much. If she comes in late, she works late to make up. She exercises a lot more than I do, which gives her that lovely figure. Sometimes she plays practical jokes."

"Any social life?"

"I don't know. She doesn't get a lot of calls at work, like some of the other employees." Kathy cocked her head at me. "You come on like a policeman, sir."

"I used to be a cop. Sorry. Didn't know it showed."

"I dated a policeman once. Up in L.A. That's one of the reasons I moved down here. He wanted to get married and I knew I couldn't handle the stress."

"A lot of women feel that way."

"Well," Kathy said, smiling. "Sally Anne's fine now and you're a hero and she'll be back in a week and I think we should enjoy what's left of the evening."

So we stopped talking for a while and she sat leaning into the breeze created by our passing and that gave me a chance to study her. The wind blew through her hair. I guessed her age at thirty-four. Her profile, I was positive, belonged on the prow of a Viking vessel. The bearded warrior-sailors would have gladly followed her into the territory of the unknown.

On the way in, I throttled down to a rhythmic chug and she asked me some questions. Where had I grown up? How had I become a private eye? What was it like in Vietnam? I answered, and she sounded interested. She asked about my parents, siblings, relatives. As I answered, I kept remembering how Mrs. Mayhew had probed me about my name, without the *k*.

"What are you thinking?"

"I was interviewed by a lady CIA operative in Vietnam. She had the same style as you. Low key. Attentive."

"I hope that's a compliment, sir."

"She didn't look illegal, if that's what you mean."

"I like it when you say that. Illegal."

As we neared the dock, she reached out, touched my arm, and scooted closer. I had this crazy vision of us standing together in an artist's painting, an adventurous pioneer couple, shoulder-to-shoulder, facing the wilderness.

"You free for dinner?"

"Sorry. I've got a date. An unbreakable one."

"Okay. How's tomorrow?"

She let go my hand. "Can I let you know?"

She hadn't said no. "Fair enough."

The connection was broken as I docked at Charley Hanrahan's. We walked to the *Laredo II* and she went to change. When she emerged, carrying her blue jacket, she was again Kathy Business, Chez Lido, Newport Beach. I helped her down the ladder. She nodded good-bye, and I was alone again.

This is something I never seem to get used to, being left by a beautiful woman. It's happened before. It always leaves the same empty feeling. When you feel empty, Uncle Walt said, bust your butt. Sweat it out.

Okay.

So I put on running shoes and shorts and headed north. Sunset was gathering as I crossed the Santa Ana River and jogged on into Huntington Beach, land of surfer-bikers. A gang of big bikes sat parked near the Main Street Pier. Their owners formed a solid core of beer guzzlers with beards and beer guts and I thought I recognized Boyd Hawley. Last summer, I'd stopped Boyd from wrecking the Blue Beat and bruising a waitress, and he'd spent a week in jail.

At the pier, I turned around and headed home.

The run took an hour and a half. A marathoner would have known how many miles, exactly, but I run to sweat and stay in balance. Counting the miles is not very Zen.

It was dark when I got back from the run. My civilian clothes were still aboard the *Laredo II*. My mind kept sliding from Eddie Hennessy to Sally Anne Sparling to Dottie Gonzales to Agent Dorn. Mostly, I thought about

Kathy Kagle. Surprise. She was waiting on the deck. She called out as I stepped aboard.

"Hello? Is that you, Murdock?"

She sat in the same director's chair where Sally Anne had sat on Friday. She'd changed clothes—white slacks, dimming in the gloom, a pale blouse that turned out to be yellow. As I came up, I saw her feet were bare.

"Welcome aboard."

"I had a change of plans. I hoped your dinner invitation was still open."

"Hey. Great." Life was suddenly better.

Down below, I showered, changed, stared at my face in the mirror, decided the beard needed trimming. I felt Kathy moving on deck, smiled a silly smile.

Monday night means clam linguini special at the Blue Beat, across the quad from my place, near the pier. We went there, in two cars. We ordered two specials and extra French bread. I drank draft beer. Kathy stayed with martinis. She continued with the questions, probing my high-school football fantasies, my first girlfriend. When I got to my undercover work as an English major for the CIA, she laughed at my tales. Her eyes were bright. Spots of red bloomed in her cheeks.

"I loved college," she said. "I never wanted to leave."

"Why did you?"

"Money. A graduate-school friend moved to Los Angeles. We'd been roommates and friends. Arlene phoned one night, from Malibu. I was working on my master's at Boulder, trying to write a novel. My professor had just bombed my plot and characters, telling me I was a hopeless romantic. It was March. The Rockies were buried under two feet of snow. Arlene had a job for me, doing industrial writing, and the temperature in L.A. was seventy-four. I was working in Denver as a cocktail waitress, living in Boulder, driving back and forth in zero weather. Some of the kids were TA's—teaching assistants—but I made twice that waiting tables. I still hadn't saved any money. I needed a new car. Arlene's job started at eighteen thousand dollars—a fortune. I kissed the snow good-bye and headed out for sunny Los Angeles. It's not a new story, exactly."

I sipped my beer and watched Kathy's eyes. They were bright with memory. She saw me watching. "What were you doing that year? Nineteen seventy-eight?"

"Building custom houses. The banks threw stones at my credit, so I went back to being a private cop."

"You built a house? Where?"

"Spyglass Hill, right here in friendly Newport. Built it for a computer hardware guy who thought he could compete with Apple and IBM. Great house, full of toys. Had a round bed, mounted on a swivel, with controls so he could minimize sunlight, moonlight."

"What did it cost?"

"The house or the bed?"

"The house."

"Almost a million. Today, two and a half."

"What happened to him?"

"He took a dive into Chapter Eleven and is now residing in Mexico."

"You like building. It shows in your face, your voice."

"Thank you, Mrs. Mayhew."

She punched my arm. "No, Murdock. I'm serious."

We walked along the beach after dinner. She took my arm and we walked with our hips touching, legs swinging in sweet rhythm. Out on the pier, the night was California soft.

94

"I'd love to build a house," she said. "Someday."

"It's a great feeling. If you can forget the banks."

"I had no idea," she said softly, "about you and your houses." And then her face was close to mine and her eyes were wide open, under the green arc light, and I saw a questioning look and then I forgot about it as we kissed with the breathlessness of discovery, bodies straining. Her left leg raised off the ground, and she leaned into me, for balance.

I was backed up against the guardrail on the pier, supported by good wood—a distinct sense of permanence. She felt me respond. Instead of pulling away, she pressed herself into me and sighed. She was soft in my arms, with insistent questing lips, and I felt the magical pressures of breast and pelvis and thigh.

Then, suddenly, she stiffened. "Oops," she whispered. "This is too darn fast!"

"Huh?"

"Too fast." She pushed herself away from me and walked a couple of steps. "I'm sorry. I don't expect you to understand."

"Try me."

"Not tonight. Walk me to the car, okay?"

We walked to her car without speaking. She unlocked it with trembling fingers and climbed in. I resisted slamming her door. "I'm sorry."

"You said that."

"I didn't mean—oh, hell." And then she drove off.

She had me going in circles, and I could still smell her perfume as I walked to the Blue Beat, where I downed too many draft beers. At the end of the evening, I tipped the waitress twenty dollars on a bill of only sixteen. Her name was Susanne. She sensed from the quantities of beer and the exorbitant tip that I was in pain.

"Girl trouble, Matt?"

"Ah-ha. Trouble doesn't cover it."

"Want a shoulder to cry on?" She handed me back the twenty.

It wasn't a bad offer, or a bad shoulder either. Susanne was twenty-five, Sally Anne's age. She was single, pretty, and temporarily sympathetic. We were pals by proximity and guys from the beach hit on her all day long and I was thinking how nice it would be to let her handle my grief for the night, but then I remembered other times with other Susannes and how using them had made me feel the next day, so I said thanks and stuffed the twenty into her hand and stumbled out into the California midnight.

7

Mrs. Hennessy woke me at seven-thirty Tuesday morning with an urgent phone call that bordered on rage. Her voice trembled as she transferred her frustration to me.

"Mr. Murdock, I'd like you to come right over!"

"What's up, Mrs. Hennessy?"

"A man just phoned with some terrible threats. He said he knew something incriminating about my husband. If I don't do exactly as he says, he'll make it public."

"What's the nature of the threat?"

"He wants money."

"How much?"

"Ten thousand dollars."

"What's he giving in return?"

"I don't know. He said not to tell the police. Or anyone. He said he'd be in touch. Can you come over, please?"

I blinked at the ceiling and sighed. There went my morning workout. "I'll just make some coffee first."

"I have coffee, Mr. Murdock."

So I rolled out and took a quick shower and called Bongo Bodette. He apologized for not finding a name and address to go with the El Señor R number from Dottie Gonzales's notebook. And he needed another day on the Hennessy finances.

"How deep is it?"

"Could be half a million," Bongo said. "Mebbe more."

"What's he been spending it on?"

"Something illegal."

"How do you know?"

"Shit, Sherlock. Feller had himself a big house, a big job, three cars, a bellyache a minute. Sooner or later he'll go wacko."

Like a lot of techies, Bongo was a closet philosopher.

Thinking positive thoughts, I drove over to Irvine and spent a couple of hours calming Mrs. Hennessy down. Her rendition of the threatening phone call kept getting vaguer with each retelling. The caller had a muffled voice. She could not detect an accent. At first, she thought it was an obscene phone call—she'd had them before, when Lizzie was in high school—so she hung up with a bang. Then he called back and started talking about her husband and the "incriminating" stuff. I didn't tell Mrs. Hennessy my suspicions about her husband and the numbered women in his secret journal. Time enough for that.

"Oh, I forgot. The man mentioned Barney. 'Don't go to your friend Ratner,' he said. 'We've got something on him, too.'"

Extortion is a crime, and I advised Mrs. Hennessy to contact the police. She said nothing doing. I told her I might not be able to help. She assured me I already was, then overfilled my coffee cup.

I used her phone to call Ratner at EJH Designs. He said he could give me ten minutes at ten-thirty. I left Mrs. Hennessy and drove to EJH Designs. When I got through the security gate, Ratner kept me waiting for half an hour. I spent some of those thirty minutes asking Ratner's secretary about Dottie Gonzales.

"Gee, I didn't know Dottie very well. She kept to herself, didn't pal around with anyone from the office. She never came to Happy Hour at RJ's."

"Who would know more about her?"

"Mr. Hennessy, I guess. They had lunch sometimes. Oh, I forgot!"

The secretary's name was Meaghan. I had an aunt on my dad's side who spelled her name the same way. Meaghan's red fingernails were an inch long. They matched her fiery lipstick. After another couple of questions, I gave up and read about the rich and famous folks in *People* magazine until Ratner buzzed me in at eleven. When I went into his office, Ratner was on the phone, feet propped on his desk, selling. He waved me to a chair. His khaki business suit reminded me of Mrs. May-hew's comment about uniforms and efficiency. Ratner wore marine dress cordovans with a spit shine. His trousers had a military crease. I hadn't been in the chair two seconds when he gave me his best corporate grin and pointed a gun at me. It was a .45, military issue. He was hanging up the phone with his left hand and using his right for the pistol. The muzzle looked big enough to walk through.

Without thinking, I rolled out of the chair, hit the floor too hard with my shoulder, and dumped over a worktable loaded with maps and blueprints and diagrams. Papers flew everywhere. I was sweating.

"Hey! Cool down there, Murdock. It's only a frigging toy!"

Ratner, grinning now at his little joke, stood up and tossed the .45 my way. It landed three feet from me and I reached out and picked it up. It was a laser toy, two hundred dollars from a snazzy gift catalog, and a pound lighter than the real thing.

"No heft." I tossed it back at Ratner, who caught it with ease.

"You always this jumpy, Murdock?"

"Only when executives in marine cordovans point guns at me."

Now he came around the desk, shaking his head and frowning. I could feel the apology coming. "Listen, I'm sorry, pal. I just got off the phone with Washington and, well—" He stopped when he saw the look in my eye. "No. No excuses. It was dumb. I love practical jokes. I should learn better."

I didn't believe he was sorry. We set the table right again and Ratner went into his executive bathroom and I sat down and thumbed through a catalog from the Sharper Image. Ratner's toy, Shooter One, was on page 27. It retailed for $199. One of the options was blowback cartridges. Hot zing.

On the next page was a Ninja suit—black blouse, black trousers, black vest. The photo showed an Oriental male model, mouth and nose covered with a Ninja scarf. The eyes held a steady Ninja Look. He held a Ninja sword and wore, according to the inset photo, official Ninja Tabi boots. Next to the Tabis was an ad for a space-age crossbow.

The wall across from me held framed plaques and degrees. One told me that Ratner had graduated from the

100

U.S. Naval Academy at Annapolis. Another, framed in black, certified Ratner as a graduate of the Harvard Business School.

Ratner came back out and sat behind his desk.

"Now what's this about?"

I told him about the threatening phone call to Christine Hennessy. "They mentioned your name. She thought you might be on the list."

He shook his head. "Crackpots. We get 'em calling here all the time. I've got an unlisted number at home." He flipped open a desk calendar and spoke without looking at me, then pressed an intercom button. "Meaghan, honey, what time am I doing lunch?"

"Twelve sharp, Mr. R. At the Rusty Pelican."

Ratner hung up, opened a drawer, stared at me, and grinned his faker's grin. I wondered if he had a Ninja suit hanging in his closet. Maybe he wore it at night, riding off to adventure on his Kawasaki Ninja 1000.

I pulled out my notebook. "What can you tell me about the SBEN?"

"Hey. Great bunch of guys. We meet every couple of weeks to sort out business problems, brainstorm new products and services. You ever been in business, Murdock?"

I caught his point. "Where do you meet?"

"At the Cote D'Azur, in Newport. We take a suite."

"Is there entertainment?"

"Like what?"

"Like dancing girls."

"Hey, this is strictly a wind-down business kind of thing. Females are verboten." He pushed his sleeve back and made a performance out of checking the time. "What does this have to do with Eddie's coin collection?"

"If I can find out where he went before he died, I might find the coins."

Ratner leaned across the desk. "Can you keep something under your hat?"

"Sure."

"I think those coins are long gone, friend. I think Eddie cashed them in a year ago, two years ago. I think Christie is wasting her money hiring you."

I reached in my shirt pocket and pulled out the page from Dottie Gonzales's notebook. "Did Dottie Gonzales call you El Señor R?"

"Who? Dottie Baby? Nah. Why should she?"

"Recognize this number?" I watched his face while I read him the phone number. The salesman's smile widened, his teeth seemed to get brighter, and there was a new tightness around his eyes.

"Nope. Sorry." Ratner stood up and started around the desk.

"Did you know where Hennessy was Wednesday afternoon?"

"Probably out raising money. He spent half his time talking to lenders. He was beautiful."

"Would he have talked to some SBEN people?"

"Eddie had his own sources. That's what made him beautiful." Ratner clapped me on the shoulder. "Stay on track, buddy. Keep after those coins and keep me up to date. I was in Naval Intelligence. I envy you your work—getting out of the office, meeting interesting people." He was steering me out.

"Were you here when the cops came yesterday?"

His first frown. "How'd you know about that?"

"You were in Naval Intelligence. You figure it out."

Anger rose up in his eyes as I turned my back and

walked out. Ratner was fibbing, trying to cover up with his usual act, but I wasn't buying. I climbed into my Plymouth and rolled the windows down and drove back through the security gate and parked down the street and waited.

When Ratner came out, I followed him. He was driving his snazzy Mercedes 450 SEL, black, with the phony little dip engineered into the roof. He took off toward Mac-Arthur. The traffic was close to gridlock, so it was easy to keep six cars in between us as a screen. When I got to the parking lot at the Rusty Pelican, Ratner's Mercedes was in the valet parking area. I found a slot big enough for the Plymouth, and went into Chicago Joe's next door just in time to see Mrs. Hennessy's Cadillac pull up. Mrs. Hennessy got out, wearing her favorite color, and walked into the restaurant. I wondered why she hadn't told me about her lunch date.

I had a sandwich and a beer. I called the 213 number for Raul, in Los Angeles. A woman answered, but she spoke only Spanish. I hung up. I called the number for El Señor R, letting it ring seven times. Nothing. I read the *Orange County Tribune*. People were killing and maiming each other everywhere with summer rage and the newspapers were reporting it with florid language so they could sell more papers.

Ratner and my client came out at two-ten. They stood talking together while the red-jacketed valets ran for the cars. Mrs. Hennessy was smiling broadly, quite a change from her usual frown. Her car came first. She gave Ratner a motherly hug and drove off.

Ratner handed the valet a tip, got into his Mercedes, and eased out of the lot. The smog was thick that after-noon as I followed his car south on Newport Boulevard to Coast Highway. He got ahead of me at St. Boniface. Then, from the bridge across Coast Highway, I spotted the Mercedes heading southeast in the right lane. It was two minutes before I made it onto Coast Highway. I cruised past Rambo's, the Ancient Mariner, and Casere's on the Coast. I made a U-turn, not the easiest maneuver on Coast Highway in high summer, and cruised back. Lucky me. Ratner and a blonde in white were coming out of Casere's. The white dress curled around her legs. She was tall, nicely built, with a sexy walk. They were heading for the Mercedes.

Tires screeching, I made a second U-turn and picked up the Mercedes at Le Club. We went south, past Reuben's and the car dealers, up the hill, past the Irvine Country Club with the high-rise shopping mall of Fashion Island to the left. There was heavy traffic in Corona del Mar. By the time I was clear, Ratner's Mercedes had disappeared. I goosed the Plymouth, which zoomed down the road at eighty. I came up over the hill just outside Laguna and thought I saw him making a left. It was a narrow street leading up into the hills. I took it; there were no other options. The street was narrow as a donkey trail in Laos. The big Plymouth took the hill with ease; they don't make cars like they used to.

The road leveled off near the top, turned left, and the name changed to Adair. I saw the Hotel Bougaineville rising up as I came around a curve. It was eight stories—too high for a building in earthquake land—with a magnificent view of the Pacific and lush Laguna Beach. I'd seen photos in the paper during the Bougaineville's construction phase. Rooms started at two hundred a day. Suites were fifteen hundred.

I parked in the shade from a palm, around the corner

from the Mercedes. The parking lot was half-full. The architect had achieved a suave Mediterranean look, white stone, red tile roofs, the intricate play of glass on glass. It reminded me of a place I'd stayed at on the French Riviera, after Vietnam, with a stunning girl named Geneviève. I estimated a hundred and fifty rooms for the elegant Bougaineville.

I was sitting in my Plymouth beneath the shade of a lofty palm tree when a black Camaro zoomed into the lot and Jancey Sheridan got out. He wore a different cowboy outfit, and as he bent down to lock the door, his jacket pulled tight and I saw the bulge of a shoulder holster. Kathy had said he was a criminal. Maybe I'd find out what kind.

Sheridan avoided the lobby and headed for a rear door painted orange. He had a key; I had to use my lock picks. The nearest elevator could only be operated by a key, and by the time I called the elevator down, he could have been on any floor. I started at the top, which was the eighth floor, without finding a trace of either Sheridan or Ratner.

Back in the parking lot, I sat in my Plymouth for a half hour before giving up and heading for home. There was a note pinned on my door from Kathy Kagle. The note said she would phone me tomorrow.

I put on my jogging clothes and went for a run. I had too many loose ends, and every time I pulled one, the carpet unraveled.

Had I really chosen to be in this business?

8

Bongo had the Hennessy report ready at noon on Wednesday, but he had to go north to Los Angeles, so Lucy June led me through it in an hour of intense detail—CDs, money markets, credit lines, mutual funds, gold futures—to the bottom line. Since October of last year, Eddie Hennessy had spent $287,000—over $187,000 in cash, another $100,000 from credit lines.

"How are you tracking the cash?"

"Tick marks." Lucy June scrolled the Macintosh screen to the bottom, where I saw three rows of slashes and two rows of check marks. "The slashes are one-thousand-dollar withdrawals. The checks are two thousand dollars. Eighty-three slashes and fifty-two checks add up to a hundred eighty-seven thousand dollars."

"How did he take the money out?"

"Express window. Hennessy had four banks. Wells Fargo. First Interstate. B of A. Barclays."

"And you're sure?"

"We just have the pattern, not the total. He cashed in six CDs, then sold two mutual funds right before the market topped out. He used forty thousand dollars to take a flyer in silver. It dropped from 9.63 to 5.4 in three hours last June. Hennessy had to cover his margin. When the cash ran out, he started using the credit lines."

"Where did it go?"

"Not into the business." She pulled up another spreadsheet. "EJH Designs has cash flow problems like you wouldn't believe. His company credit lines were drawn to the limit. The business owes half a million to banks."

"Any luck with the gold coins?"

She pulled a sheet of paper out of a manila folder with my name on it. "He recorded some of the coin purchases. It's hard to tell how much he kept in his head. The guy was good with numbers. Every guy's got his little hoard, right? This figure, for thirty-two thousand, was for some 1912 French Roosters. This one for forty-five Maple Leafs at three hundred fifty dollars a pop. There's no record of him selling any."

"He could have sold them and not recorded the sales."

"Sure."

"What about house payments?"

She nodded. "The mortgage is prepaid, up through December. It's thirty-five hundred a month, a hefty piece of change. He owes money on a Porsche, which he leased. On a Cadillac Seville. And on a Toyota."

The Toyota was the daughter's car. I did not relish telling Christine Hennessy the bad news. "How much in the bank accounts?"

Lucy June pulled out a spreadsheet filled with numbers. "There's a household account with five thousand. A personal account for Mr. Hennessy with fifteen hundred. And a personal account for Mrs. Hennessy, four thousand."

"And that's it? That's what's liquid?"

"Three thousand in a money market, Capital Preservation II, a good outfit. He owes just under ninety thousand on his personal credit lines."

The phone rang. Lucy June handed me the manila folder marked "EJH" and went to answer it. I moved through the columns, all neatly printed. Halfway through, I found a column of names. At the top of the page the computer had printed the word "Search," followed by "Lido":

Club Lido
Casere's Lido
Chez Lido
Serpentine Lido
Lido Enterprises
Lido Investitures
Lido Answering Service
Lido Random Access
Lido Cafe
Lido Dry Cleaning
Lido Appreciations
Lido Illusions
Lido Landing
Lido Frontiers
Lido Explorations
Lido Futures
Lido Motels
Lido Escort

Lido Enterprises was the place with the high-fence credit limit. I showed Lucy June the list.

"Where did this come from?"

"Bongo loves fooling around with his modem. He's a mischief maker for data bases." She pointed at a code in the upper left-hand corner. "This stuff came from a Newport Beach city directory. They just encoded it a month ago."

She closed the EJH folder and handed it to me. I handed her seventy-five dollars, thanked her, and drove slowly home. I sat on the deck for thirty minutes, drinking a Bud and thinking how I would break the news to Mrs. Hennessy. She was broke. Unless there was life insurance, she would have to change her Turtle Rock lifestyle.

Since no insights came, I strolled across the quad to the Blue Beat, where I ordered more beer, and after that a hamburger with well-done fries. The fries restored me. I was finishing the hamburger, my eyes glazing over at the numbers on Bongo's printouts, when Kathy Kagle appeared in the doorway. She wore a yellow dress with a belt, a light blue scarf around her neck. The dress, while pretty, was all business. So was the briefcase. I waved, closed my folder, and stood up. She looked beautiful.

"I went to find you."

"Here I am."

"I sat on your deck. In the sun. Lovely spot. Then I remembered you hung out here."

"Want a drink?"

"Love it."

"Martini?"

"Beer. It's hot on that deck of yours."

We worked on one pitcher, and then one more. She apologized for the other night. "Moods," she said. "I wish I could tell you they won't come again."

"You look criminal today."

"Is that better than illegal? Or worse?"

"Illegal makes my pulse race. Criminal, well . . ."

I smiled and she smiled back, and then she suggested we walk across the quad to my place. "Autumn approaches, and after that winter. I'd like to get some sun."

Walking across, I kept waiting for another mood swing. We stopped at a parking meter to up the time limit on her Buick. She unlocked the wagon, put the briefcase inside, and brought out a green canvas satchel. "I took the afternoon off. Did you have plans?"

I had the Hennessy report. "Whatever it was just went on hold."

I waited in the living room while she used the bathroom to change. She left the bathroom door open about four inches. From the bathroom, I could hear silken female rustlings, water running, muffled thuds as her shoes hit the floor. I changed into khaki shorts, put Bongo's manila folder on the coffee table, and went barefoot into the kitchen. I was just closing the fridge when she came out. The bikini was blue, revealing, sexy against her deep tan. She looked like a model in a magazine ad.

"Do we keep drinking, or what?"

"We keep drinking."

Kathy led the way outside, where we arranged big towels on the chaise longues. The sun was hot and I figured the temperature in the high eighties. She told me about her father.

"My dad was an artist and a scholar and a seeker. We

lived outside the town of Fort Collins. He taught art for a while at CSU. He hated being dependent. He taught me about living in the moment, about being yourself no matter what."

"Good lessons."

She'd sold her first piece of writing to the *Denver Post* when she was a junior English major at Colorado. CU, she called it. She still had the check, framed, on her office wall. It had been a memory piece called "Flags I Remember," for the Fourth of July issue. "I thought the world was open to my words," Kathy said. "Boy, was I set up for a shock. In a year, I had enough rejection slips to paper this whole house. Sometimes an editor would write me a note. 'Sorry. Not for us.' So I waited tables."

"And now here you are, pals with the Mayhews."

"Not really pals. She let me decorate her house." Kathy paused. "I decided not to wrestle her about the colors. Everything was either white or gold. She's very rich, buys her clothes in Paris, but her taste gags."

"Where did she make her money?"

"She married it. Some banker, I think, back East."

"What happened to him?"

"It was your typical June-December marriage. He died, and along came Landis. Or perhaps Landis came along, and then he died. Angela likes younger men."

"Does Landis have money?"

"It's hard to tell. He talks about his family back in the South as if they owned Tara."

"Scarlett's place?"

"Um."

"Where did you live in L.A.?"

"Malibu." She drained her beer, set it down, and the

movement made her bikini top drift lower. She closed her eyes and sighed. She must have felt me watching because she opened her eyes and smiled an easy smile. "You like?"

"I like."

"I was ugly, growing up. I was awkward and overweight."

"Hard to believe."

"Not for me. Inside, there's still a fat kid getting fatter on Oreos." She yawned, raising tan arms above her head. "When I was sixteen, things started to happen. When I was seventeen, the boys noticed. A boy tried to rape me on our first date. I fought him off, but I was scared of men—you're all so strong, comparatively—so I wouldn't go out, except with a gang of girls, even in college."

"Was it better in college?"

"I felt like prey."

"Want another beer?"

"Um. But first, I need the girl's room."

She retied the halter straps and we walked inside together. How many beers? Six for me? Seven? How many for her? I knew I was ahead. It was a lazy Wednesday and I was letting Kathy Kagle steer the day. She came out of the bathroom, looking willowy and desirable, and my mouth got a little dry watching her.

"My turn for the room."

She touched my arm as I went past. Her eyes were smiling. When I came out, she was studying my unfinished wall unit.

"This is beautiful work, Murdock."

"Thanks. I'm slow."

"But good."

Back on the deck, she changed subjects. "You in the mood to counsel a girl about money trouble?"

"I'm not so hot with money myself."

"It's Angela. I owe her money."

"How much?"

"A hundred and forty thousand."

"Quite a bundle."

"It's complicated. Angela hates to be alone, just one of her many phobias. She needs people around her, desperately. A year ago, when I was decorating her house, I had some cash flow problems. Angela picked up on it right away when I couldn't pay for that gold cloth and had to ask for advance payments. So she made me a business loan."

"Interest?"

"One point over prime. If I can't pay, she gets a third of the business."

"Have you paid any back?"

"Oh, sure. The original loan was for one sixty. She tells me she doesn't need the money. But she keeps inviting me to these parties."

"You could trade places with Midge Talbot. She's dying to get in that circle."

"She's nice. I liked her."

"Why don't you say no? To the parties?"

"I did, a couple of times. Angela didn't speak to me for a week, and then we had lunch and she talked about *not* calling in the loan, of course meaning the reverse, that she was about to call it in. I know what she wants. She wants me . . . as part of her admiring court. There are lots of parties—last Sunday was an example—and they eat up time and my creative juices. I haven't written anything in months. I don't have time to draw. The worst part is if I don't make the business hum I can't make the money to pay her back."

"Vicious circle," I said.

"Exactly."

"And you think she wants it this way?"

"She's hurt a couple of other women. One's an artist who does beautiful work . . . or used to. The other one ran a natural healing clinic in South Laguna. But last month she closed her center and left town."

"What did Mrs. Mayhew do?"

"Something vicious. I don't know the details." Kathy shook her head and I saw a tear running down her cheek.

"We could dynamite her fountain. As a sign of rebellion." I put a hand on Kathy's shoulder and she moved toward me.

"I got myself into it. I'll get myself out." She paused. "At times like these, I wish my dad was around, just to talk to."

"So Friday night, when we called about Sally Anne, you were sitting at Mrs. Mayhew's feet."

"Good metaphor. She insisted on coming along. She's seen Sally Anne, and I'm sure she'd love to recruit her for her endless parties."

"She said she didn't know Sally Anne."

"Of course. Why should she admit it?"

"Something's been bugging me."

"Um?" She really wasn't listening.

"We called your answering service on Friday, and they relayed the message to Mrs. Mayhew's, right?"

"Yes."

"It took me less than ten minutes to get dressed and get down to the lobby. When I got there, Midge was talking to Mrs. Mayhew and you were already at the information booth."

"I don't follow."

"It takes twenty minutes to drive from Mrs. Mayhew's to St. Boniface. So who else called?"

Kathy walked to the railing. I got up off the chaise. She leaned on the railing for a moment before turning to stare at me through wide eyes, and I could tell my question had made her nervous. Her face became hard for just a second and I thought, She's leaving now, here comes a mood change and an exit line. But she fooled me. The hard expression turned soft and sensual and she inched closer until we were touching and then she put her face up for a kiss, and no sooner had our lips met than she opened her mouth to take my tongue. We hung that way for a long moment, unaware of the world passing by on its way to the beach, and then someone down below broke the mood with a catcall.

"Whoo-ee!"

We broke. I glared down at the kid in the knee-length surfing pants.

"Don't go away, okay?" She brushed my lips with hers and walked into the house. I was turned on. She hadn't answered me about her trip on Friday night from Mrs. Mayhew's to the hospital. When she came to the screen door and looked out from the dimness inside, I decided to forget my worries about travel time, or at least set them aside, because the bikini was gone and now her only garment was a bath towel around her waist.

"You didn't go away," she said.

115

It was a clear invitation. I moved to the screen door. She stepped back as I opened it. When I came in, she was standing in the center of the room, wearing only a white towel, and when I stopped, she smiled and gave the towel a little tug and it fell away and she was naked. Backlit from the afternoon sun, she was the same shimmery copper tone all over.

"I can hear you thinking, Murdock."

"Call me Matt."

"I can hear you thinking, Matt."

Enough talk. I moved to her, but she moved away. I reached out for her, but she gave a little laugh and danced out of reach, putting the sofa between us. Her eyes were on fire and her smile was mischievous. This was one mood swing I liked. I caught her wrist after a couple of more turns around the sofa and pulled her to me. The kiss was good, and she managed to stay close while she worked loose my belt buckle and top button. When the shorts were off, she said, "Hmm," and then she said, "Music," and we walked giggling to my ancient stereo, where she kneeled down until she found a scratchy recording of *Bolero*.

"I love corn."

"I love you."

"That sounds practiced, Murdock. Too practiced, you rascal!" She came into my arms again, and after another long kiss she led me to the bedroom. "Illegal, am I?" She was punching me in the ribs, trying to tickle me. "Criminal, am I?"

And that's the way we spent the afternoon. And the evening. I remember animal sounds, salty sweat taste, the smell of Kathy's hair, moans of pleasure.

Toward midnight, we had a snack in bed. Crackers and cheese, a bottle of wine.

"Murdock?"

"Yes."

"I had a lovely time."

"Then you can call me Matt."

"All right. Matt. I've stayed away from men for a while. Quite a while. I hate feeling helpless."

I tried to pat her shoulder, but she shoved my hand away and rolled away from me and shut herself in the bathroom.

In the night, I woke to find her side of the bed empty. Light came from under the door. My legs were unsteady, but my heart was strong. I opened the door. Kathy sat on my sofa, reading the Hennessy folder. She wore one of my blue Levi shirts. Half a glass of Napa Zinfandel sat on the table, near her right foot. It was a magazine model's pose. She had left the shirt unbuttoned.

"Enjoying your read?"

She closed the folder. "Sorry. I'm the world's worst snoop."

I took the folder off the table and stood there, looking down at her. "Did you know Hennessy?"

"No. How could I?"

"You could have met at one of Mrs. Mayhew's endless parties."

"No." She sipped her wine and stared into the distance. "We didn't."

"Maybe you decorated his house. It's a big place, up in Turtle Rock."

"No. I would have remembered."

"You know how Hennessy died?"

117

"No." Her voice was a low whisper.

"He died in bed, probably with a woman. Then someone moved his body to a supermarket parking lot. When the cops found him, around midnight, he wasn't wearing his wedding ring. They're calling it death by natural causes, and someone high up in the local government has put a hold on the autopsy."

"Why are you telling me this?"

"Just running one of my cases by you, since you picked it out. Hennessy weighed two twenty. It would take two men to move him. Dead bodies seem heavier."

Kathy set down her wineglass and stood up. "I said I was sorry." She brushed past me into the bedroom. I could hear her moving around. The light came on in the bathroom, and then the door closed, all the way. I sat down on the sofa and thought about my next move. She'd made me suspicious and then we'd made love and then she'd read the dossier and now I was pissed.

She came out wearing the yellow dress. Her face was cold, without expression. Her eyes looked like the eyes of a stone statue.

"Thanks for the beer. Thanks for everything."

I waited until she was almost to the door before saying anything. "I saw your boy Jancey Sheridan yesterday."

She stopped with her hand on the latch and half turned back to regard me over her shoulder. "Jancey? Where?"

"At the Bougaineville, that fancy hotel above Laguna. He was driving a Camaro and packing a big pistol in a shoulder holster."

"Why *are* you telling me this?"

"Just thought you'd like to know."

"Well, you're wrong. You're wrong about a lot of things."

And then she opened the door and walked out into the night. The time was two in the morning. I listened to her footsteps going down the stairs, and then I went to the door and watched her cross the quad toward the parking meters. She unlocked the Buick and got in. The car cranked awhile before starting. Headlights came on.

And then Kathy Kagle drove away, leaving me alone with my suspicions.

The detective engine chugged along. Sometimes it's hard to shut off.

9

The Hennessy case broke Thursday morning when Mrs. Hennessy phoned me in hysterics. The time was eight-oh-two. I had just rolled over to finish my dream about Kathy Kagle, who was walking away from me wearing a long white dress, staring at me over her right shoulder. Her eyes were sightless, like the eyes of a marble statue. In the dream, I was strapped on a marble bed on the roof of Mrs. Mayhew's house on Balboa. A party was going on downstairs. Kathy waved, a bell rang, and I clawed my way out of sleep as she vanished down an endless flight of stairs.

"They want ten thousand dollars, Mr. Murdock! Do you understand? Ten thousand dollars!"

"Who?"

"These people. They mailed *filth* to my home! They used a messenger service! I wanted to burn them, incinerate them! How soon can you get here?"

"What kind of photos?"

"Please, Mr. Murdock. Not over the phone!"

"All right. I'm on my way."

It was almost nine when I got to Turtle Rock, but there was no breeze, and the weatherman on KNX said inland Orange County would hit ninety-five today. At the Hennessy place on Orchard, the garage door was down and the house looked buttoned up. The door opened before I was out of the car, and Mrs. Hennessy appeared on the brick walk, wearing blue slacks and a silk blouse. Her face had a tormented look. In her hand was a plain brown envelope with the snappy orange and green logo of Overnight X-Press.

"This filth came right to my door, Mr. Murdock. A man in a truck actually smiled when he asked me to sign for this! I thought it was a communication from the bank. Imagine my absolute horror when I opened the package and found—"

She thrust the package into my hands and I followed her inside. I handed her Bongo's manila folder and she dropped it on the coffee table and lit a cigarette. I sat on the sofa while I looked at the contents of her brown envelope. There were a dozen photos of a naked man, heavyset, thinning hair, and two women wearing masks.

It was an anonymous bedroom. The focus was on the activity in the bed. I could hear Mrs. Hennessy breathing in moral outrage as I went through the photographs. Eddie Hennessy's face was recognizable in each photo. The masks of the women were dark leather, with Velcro slits for eyes, mouth, and nose. One woman wore see-through harem pantaloons and a black choker with a chain attached. The other wore standard S & M garb—black leather vest, gloves up to the elbows, garter belt, boots.

Was one of them Number 18, from Hennessy's writings? Was one Number 6?

"Well, do something!"

"What are you supposed to do with the money?"

"Get it together . . . in small bills. I shall be contacted."

She handed me a crumpled note. The words had been typewritten, all caps, several misspellings. She would be told about delivery of the money. She was not to call the police. Any false move, they'd send the photos to the papers, and to her husband's business acquaintances and financial supporters.

"You must help me."

I sat back. Bongo's folder lay closed on the coffee table. "Like I said yesterday, it's a job for the police."

"If this got out, about Eddie, I could not lift my head in this town."

"Was it the same voice?"

"Yes. Muffled. I think so."

We went over it again. She couldn't face the police. Too public, she said. Too embarrassing, having outsiders know. I wanted the cops because there was not much I could do. They had the manpower, the routines for handling the phones. Her tone of voice made me to understand it was my moral obligation to bail her out. I hate moral obligation.

We ended in a Mexican standoff. I said I'd continue working and hope for something to break. Then I went through the financial folder with her. She had trouble concentrating, but when she saw the bottom line, Mrs. Hennessy threw the folder down.

"Other women!" she snorted. "All that money?"

The numbers said her husband had thrown away over a quarter of a million on "other women." Her outrage filled the room. For the moment, the gold coins were forgotten. She put her face in her hands and cried. Angry tears, helpless tears.

"Let me know if they call."

"You aren't going?"

"And don't give them any money."

"Of course not."

The daughter's Toyota pulled into the driveway as I was leaving, and Lizzie Hennessy got out from behind the wheel and stared at me with hands on hips. She wore short shorts and a tight blue T-shirt. She'd been working on her tan.

"Not a word to Lizzie."

I nodded and shook Mrs. Hennessy's hand. "I'll be in touch." It was all I had to say.

They stood together watching me as I started the Plymouth. I drove home, working through possible scenarios. Back at my place, I made a list of what I knew about the Hennessy case.

Hennessy and masked hookers.
Posh hotel? Motel?
Cash payments.
Wife angry.
$200-$250K out the door. Upscale operation.
Four bank accounts.
Missing coin collection. Missing secretary.
Business has cash flow problems. Half a million.
Heart attack, probably in hooker's bed.
Driven to parking lot by phantom helper.
Body, too heavy for a woman to lift.
Shakedown, connected to hookers.

Who was the mastermind?
Hookers need pimp. Or madame.
Mob connection? Vegas?

I kept working on the list, running into dead ends. I felt like a rat in a maze. Kathy was on my mind. I opened a beer, but didn't finish it. Mrs. Hennessy called twice, with no news. I wondered how she was handling it with her daughter. I ate lunch. Around five, Captain Tommy called from his Newport office. He wanted to meet at the *Laredo II* in fifteen minutes. His voice, usually so calm and cool and controlled, was nervous.

I got into my jogging clothes and made it to Bay Avenue seven minutes before Captain Tommy. He didn't shake hands. Instead, he shoved an envelope at me. It sported the orange and green logo of Overnight X-Press. "This could ruin my life, partner."

Shakedown City.

Tommy hurried below for beer while I went through the contents of his envelope. There were six photos of Tommy and a masked hooker in S & M garb. The note demanding ten grand in small bills was typed on a typewriter, all caps, with several words misspelled. Tommy came out with two beers. He wore shorts, deck shoes, a striped pullover. His face was pale as ashes. I remembered he'd made a crack about women and masks the day Sally Anne had jumped overboard.

"Can you help me, partner?"

"I can try."

"What can you do?"

"It's a snake's nest. I need to get inside, shoot up the place, crowd whoever's behind this, and try to rescue the videotapes."

124

"What videotapes?"

"The ones they shot of you, so they could pull off these stills."

"Ah, God. What a mess." He drank some beer and shook his head sadly. "What if they carry through with their threat? About making things public?"

"That's the chance you take. How do you make contact?"

"We have this club, some guys, called the SBEN. You meet girls there, make a date for the next day, the day after. The girls are clean, checked out by a physician— that's part of the price. The day of your date, you call a number and they tell you where to meet. After the pickup, you drive to a hotel and have a party. It's all pretty harmless."

"Expensive?"

"A thousand for the afternoon. Two thousand for a night and a day. Most of the guys can't get away for that long. There are out-of-town trips. Do you need to know this?"

"Could you get me in there?"

"I might. I recommended a client from Scottsdale . . . last March. His credit's cleared. We could use his code name."

"What code name?"

"Mr. Orange."

I did my best to keep a straight face. "Jesus, Tommy. How long have you been into this?"

"A year. Thirteen months." His face was white as he stood up quickly and headed downstairs. The door to the head closed. I could hear him throwing up. When he came back, his face was pale and sweaty.

"The same hotel?"

"Usually."

"Has it got a name?"

"The Bougaineville. It's a fancy place in Laguna."

I remembered Ratner with the blonde on Tuesday.

"What was your code name?"

"Mr. Blue."

It was getting better by the minute. "And the girls have numbers, right?"

Tommy stared at me. "How'd you know?"

"Lucky guess. You get drugs for this price?"

"If you want."

"You into that, too?"

"Hey, I can handle it, partner. No sweat."

I tapped the photos. "What's her number?"

"Twenty-seven." His voice was so choked he could barely speak.

"They took these in the Bougaineville?"

"Yes. They've got a master suite."

"Any idea where the camera might be?"

"In the wall. Christ. I don't know, Matt. All these questions you're hammering at me. I'm in bloody shock."

If I used Tommy to get inside, I might get my hands on the videotapes of Eddie Hennessy. "Okay, strategy time. Who's the client from Scottsdale?"

"Melville. J. D. Melville."

"What's he look like?"

"About your size, early fifties. More gray in the hair. He wore cowboy clothes the last time, a white suit." Tommy peered at me. "I got him a date with Number Thirteen, but she's not around anymore."

"Where'd she go?"

He shrugged. "Somewhere else. Great-looking girl, too."

"Well, let's go for it. You get me a grand and make the contact. I'll bring out those tapes."

"Man, if this gets out, Midge and I are finished. Over. Done with."

I thought of Midge in her orange party dress, working the crowd at Mrs. Mayhew's for Tommy's insurance business. "Maybe you'll get lucky."

"Jeez, I hope so." He sat there rocking in the deck chair for a couple of minutes before trudging off to the pay phone on the dock. The sun was pale orange on the horizon. Tommy was a fool, thinking he could keep this from Midge. She was no dummy.

In five minutes, Tommy came back with news. Mr. Orange had a date with Number 6 for three tomorrow afternoon.

"Who's Number Six?"

"A blonde. You'll go wild."

"This is a business trip, you dork."

"I know. I know. Just recommending the merchandise. It's first-class."

He walked me through procedure again. I'd pick up the thousand from his office tomorrow morning. He'd give me the number to call for the pickup spot. Now that he'd made the decision, he was working hard, talking intensely, eyes flashing, sweat beads on his forehead. I saw why he was good at the insurance game. He knew how to close a sale.

"What if you can't get those tapes?"

"One thing at a time, okay?"

"I don't want Midge to know."

"She may find out."

"I know. Christ, don't you think I've been living with that?"

"Yeah. I think you have. Want another beer?"

"Okay, sure. I could use a line."

"Forget it."

Tommy glared at me. "You're a real puritan, aren't you?"

We sat there for a minute without talking and I thought about my uniform for tomorrow. A white cowboy suit and a hat to match. Cowboy boots, a hand-tooled belt, and the ankle holster with the .32 belly-gun. Call me Mr. Orange.

"Who do you think runs this operation?"

Tommy took a sip of beer before answering. "There's been some speculation about that among the guys. About every four months, they bring in new girls from somewhere, so there must be other operations. The smart money says it's run from Las Vegas."

"The Lucianos were into hookers, back in the seventies."

"I need to explain something, so you'll understand. I was just knocking some edges off my stress profile. It was easy, painless, safe. The girls are fantastic and for a while you just forget what a shithole the world is and dive in. They take your money and they dish out pleasure and fun in return and they aren't whining after you to buy something to impress the goddamn neighbors. And the tab helps because it encourages you to grab your fun with both hands, not to analyze the goddamn organizational structure." Tommy stood up. "Good luck tomorrow."

"Thanks."

We shook hands. I watched him walk away, toward his Volvo Turbo. I thought about going out for a run, decided against it, and opened another beer.

Might as well enjoy the boat while it lasted.

10

That night when I tried calling Kathy, I kept getting her answering service. I left two messages, one around eight, the other around ten. She did not return my call, so I tried again the next morning. I wanted to ask her about Jancey Sheridan and his business at the Bougaineville.

"Miss Kagle is not picking up. Would you care to leave a message?"

"I tried that. Has she checked in since ten o'clock?"

"I'm afraid I can't tell you that, sir. Would you care to leave a message?"

"Sure. Have her call Murdock." I gave out my number again.

"All right, sir. I have the message."

After a leisurely breakfast of sausage and eggs, I dropped by Captain Tommy's office to pick up an envelope containing twelve hundred dollars in cash. A thousand would go to Lido Enterprises—Tommy's payment for fooling around on his wife—and the other two hundred would go for my disguise. I decided not to phone Webby Smith about our lunch date. He was good at reading my moods. The Bougaineville was in his town. I didn't want him asking questions.

I rented a Lincoln at the airport. Their fleet had no Jaguars, and the single BMW was in the shop. Driving the big suave Lincoln gave me a feel for the corporate shuffle. Murdock, fat cat. Then I rented a cowboy uniform—a white twill western suit, a string tie, and a white cowboy hat.

Back at my place, I showered, edged the beard, and took my time dressing. At two o'clock, I called Lido Enterprises and found out my rendezvous was at Casere's, where I had seen Ratner and his blonde. I put a coil of heavy twine in my jacket pocket.

I strapped the ankle holster on and wondered if I needed more firepower. A .32 snub-nose hits like a drunk bumblebee. You have to aim for ultimate vulnerability. The cylinder held six shots. I amplified that with two speed-loaders, on the other ankle.

Armed, I strolled across the quad for a final beer at the Blue Beat. My nerves were edgy, taut, but I resisted a second beer. I'd had the same edgy feeling in Vietnam, just before an attack.

At three twenty-two, I sat on a stool in Casere's bar, sipping a second beer. The bar curved in a half-moon around the room, to wind up at a long wall of windows that looked out onto Newport Bay. The bartender could have doubled for the bodybuilder in that TV show about the sympathetic Hulk. He had dark hair, cropped short like a marine, a thick neck, and cold blue eyes. He wore a Casere's T-shirt.

There was a skinny cocktail waitress in shorts and a white Casere's T-shirt. In one corner, three suits drank Margaritas and watched a baseball game.

The Dodgers were playing the Cardinals in Los Angeles, a situation which did not involve my Braves. I had the feeling the waitress and Mr. Muscles knew why I was there.

At three twenty-eight, the door opened, and a tall female figure stood for a moment in the doorway, with the light from the parking lot behind her. The three suits even turned away from the ball game to watch. For a moment there, I thought it was Sally Anne. She had the same model's body, the same swaying walk. But then the door swung shut and she came inside and I saw she was not Sally Anne, but Ratner's blonde. I grinned at that and hoped they were shaking Ratner down.

She had a sharp face, with cover-girl cheekbones. She wore a green skirt set off nicely by a silky white blouse with shoulder pads. The walk made you watch her hips, then travel down to slim legs. Pretty enough for *Playboy*. Tall enough for *Vogue*.

She came to the bar, smiling. "Mr. Orange, I presume."

"Yes, ma'am."

She held out a soft hand. "I'm Number Six."

I was impressed. Number 6 was attractive, instantly magnetic. Just being close to her made you understand what kept Eddie Hennessy coming back with his checkbook ready to fire. And Captain Tommy. And Barney Ratner.

"Would you like to stay here? Have a quiet drink? Or are you a man with a schedule?"

"That's me, little lady. Places to go and them jet airplanes to catch."

I paid the bill. I was happy to pay it. I was happy to walk out of there, with Number 6's arm through mine, the smell of her perfume close. For a split second, she made me forget why I was there.

On the way to the rented Lincoln, she held my arm, asked if she could drive. It was a rented car—why not? I unlocked the driver's door and handed her the keys. By the time I walked around, she had the air conditioner going and the stereo tuned to hard rock. The green skirt was up, showing pretty knees, flashy stockings, and much thigh.

"You sound like you're from the South, Mr. Orange."

"You-all got a good ear, honey."

Number 6 punched it, cleaving the traffic, sixty-five miles an hour, seventy-five. She drove with both hands on the wheel, racetrack style. Her narrow model's face glowed. When she braked, more leg appeared from beneath the skirt. At the light on Jamboree, she reached over to feel my bicep. "Mmmm. You keep in shape, Mr. Orange."

"Working them oil rigs, ma'am."

The light changed and we started south again, toward Corona del Mar. "So many men your age have gone to fat."

"All them pressures," I said. "In the bidness world."

She nodded. An understanding hooker.

In the parking lot outside the Bougaineville, she asked me for the money, and I counted out nine hundred dollars in twenties.

"You're short a hundred, Mr. Orange."

"Whups. You're right." I gave her a hayseed grin, handed over five more twenties. She pulled my face close and kissed me, expertly, and I found my mind drifting from my mission. Maybe it was the thrill of the unknown. Maybe it was the girl, so pretty in her crisp skirt and filmy blouse. Maybe it was the price tag—you get what you pay for. It was a trained kiss, a feathery brush like a butterfly's wings, but building quickly to insistent urging. She was a good little actress. I wondered who'd trained her.

She was a pro. She knew I was aroused. With a playful squeeze, she led me around behind the Bougaineville to the orange metal door. She opened it with a key from a huge gold ring. We took the special elevator to the sixth floor. Holding hands, we walked down the thickly carpeted corridor. I had an urge to ask her about Ratner. What was his name? Mr. Purple? Mr. Pink? Mr. Gold? She unlocked the door to 611, a corner suite. Before going in, I checked the doors on either side. To the left was a connecting room, number 609.

Inside, I stood in the alcove, surveying the room, while she switched on the giant-screen TV where a blue movie was already in progress. It showed a simple woodland scene, two naked girls on a blanket, doing X-rated unmentionables to a heavily muscled man. The sound track was heavy rock, loud and obvious.

Pulling me into the suite, she kissed me some more, swiveled her pelvis into mine, thrust her chest my way. "Unhitch!" she ordered. "Do me!" I snapped open her brassiere. It was white and sheer. Hips bumping to the music, she went to the bathroom. The lock clicked softly. The champagne popped open like high-class stuff. In front of me, the room widened into a sitting room with a French love seat and a rosewood secretary. French doors opened out onto a balcony. Beyond that, the sea. The headboard was the one in the extortion photos.

There were three possibilities for the camera. Number

one was in the wall separating the bathroom from the bedroom. Number two was behind the mirror near the doorway. Number three was behind the TV screen.

I filled two beakers with champagne and carried them across the room. When I knocked on the bathroom door, the lock clicked and the door opened. Smiling, Number 6 looked out. Smiling back, I held up the champagne. She drank half a glass. "Yum," she said. "I'll just be one more minute."

With my jacket off and my shirt unbuttoned, I walked around the suite, sipping champagne. I turned down the volume on the TV and surveyed the angle from here to the bed. In the extortion stills, Hennessy had been on his back, head near the bed, and the camera had caught him from the left. Captain Tommy had assumed the missionary position, and the camera had caught his right side. One camera had to be behind the TV screen.

The bathroom door opened and out walked Number 6. She wore bright red bikini panties, white mesh Madonna stockings, a white garter belt, and a sheer white see-through bra. Her champagne glass was empty. Her left hand hid something behind her back.

"Why, Mr. Orange. You're still decent."

I grinned. "Nervous, I reckon."

She gave me a hooker's understanding smile. Then she grabbed the champagne bottle by the neck and walked toward me. Standing close, she filled our champagne glasses.

"You just let me, okay?"

She started to help me off with my shirt, and I half walked, half fell back toward the alcove.

"Hey!" she said, and a black leather object dropped from her hand.

The leather mask. Time to go to work.

I danced her into the alcove and locked her wrists behind her back. Eyes wide, she struggled. "Damn you! What the—?" She was stronger than she looked. Hoping we were out of camera range, I stuffed the mask into her mouth, at the same time blocking a knee aimed at my crotch. She scratched my face. I clipped her lightly behind the neck and she went limp.

Working fast, I tied her wrists with the twine from my pocket. I roped my necktie between her clenched teeth, so she couldn't spit the mask out. I moved back into camera range and found the gold key ring in the bathroom tucked in her purse next to Tommy's twenties. I pocketed the twenties, then stepped to the bathroom door and called out. "Hey, darlin', here I come!"

Then I moved quickly across the room, past Number 6, who was still out. I opened the door and pulled out the .32. The corridor was empty. From behind the door to 609, I could hear voices talking in that unmistakable sportscaster cadence, a play-by-play of a summer ball game. The key ring had a key with the number 609 on it. I unlocked the door to the room.

A man was on his back on a white sofa, watching the game. He wore white pants, a striped shirt, and tennis shoes. His back was to me and the door. In his right hand was a can of beer. He heard the door open and spoke without looking at me. His voice had the lilting uncertainty of the foreign speaker who has learned enough English to get by.

"That's about time, Donald. I was be—"

I was halfway to him when he turned and saw me. He was a dark kid in his mid-twenties, dressed Mediterranean-style, with his shirt open to show a heavy mat of black hair and a snazzy gold chain around his neck. He saw the gun, jumped up, and bolted for the connecting door. I tripped him. He fell against a wall. Something went crunch. His eyes fluttered as he went out. Behind me, two video cameras were rolling. The kid moaned. Dragging him with me, I checked the connecting door, which led to a room filled with portable metal shelves. The shelves contained rows of videotapes.

The kid wore a white mesh belt, which I used to tie his hands. I ripped the shirt off, tore it into strips, and got him hog-tied. His wallet contained three hundred in cash, two credit cards, and a driver's license that said he was Tadash Farouki, currently residing in Huntington Beach.

The videotapes were in alphabetical order—Mr. Argentine, Mr. Barclay, Mr. Blue, Mr. Brown, Mr. Calvados, Mr. Contrarian, Mr. Crocker, Mr. Dollar, Mr. Fargo, etc. After the name was a date, then an indication of the services performed. "Mr. Blue, April 3, full session." An IBM computer was in the far corner of the room, next to the bed. There were two plastic cases of computer disks—Customer Data File 202.1, 202.2, 202.3, and so on—which I tossed into a pillowcase. I also tossed in all the tapes that said "Mr. Brown" (that was Hennessy) and "Mr. Blue" (that was Captain Tommy).

Tadash watched me from his place on the floor.

"Who runs this operation?"

"You are going to be one very sad person," he said.

"So are you, Tadash. You can talk to me. Or you can talk to the cops."

He spat at me through stained teeth, but the spit didn't reach. It was not Tadash's day.

There were two phones in the room, one white, one red. I picked up the red phone, a red light winked at me, and a woman's voice said, "This is Lido Central. How is your afternoon going?"

"Oh, veddy fine," I said, and hung up.

The white phone went through the Bougaineville switchboard. I used it to call Webby Smith at the Laguna Beach PD.

"Lieutenant Smith is unavailable at this time. This is Sergeant Bentley. Can I help you?"

"This is Murdock, Sarge. If you'll run a unit up to the Bougaineville, you'll find what remains of a vice operation up to its elbows in a heavy sting. My guess is it will implicate some of Orange County's big names, so if I were you, I'd get here and seal it off before the press arrives."

"I'll get the lieutenant on the horn, Murdock. You stay put."

"Yes, Sergeant."

I should have left the scene with my cassette tapes, but instead I stuck around to bust up the video equipment with a hotel chair. I did it for Eddie Hennessy. It was expensive stuff, Japanese-made, and from its size I guessed it could have been used to shoot TV dramas. Every swing of the chair got me madder at Tommy Talbot.

"Stupid!" I growled. "Dumb. Dumb. Dumb."

The equipment shattered nicely. I was sweating as old Tadash inched his way to the door of the other room to watch me with an expression of horror. I finished wrecking the number one camera and was starting on number two when the door opened and reinforcements walked in. It was one of the suits from Casere's. He carried a six-pack and a striped tub of Colonel Sanders' finest. When he saw me, he dropped the tub, spewing chicken everywhere. He was going for his piece when I shot him in the leg, above the knee. He was a short, stocky guy, with lots of staying power. He didn't drop the piece, so I ran at him and kicked it away. He made a grab for my legs, but I hammered him in the ear. That doubled him over. Wondering who'd heard the shot, I kicked the door closed.

I was short of breath as I used the phone line to wrap up his hands. I dropped his wallet into the pillowcase. His gun was a snub-nosed .38. I dropped it in, too.

"Who the fuck are you?"

"The sandman. And I'm putting this operation to sleep."

"You're dead, Jack."

I stuffed his tie in his mouth, locked up, and went next door. Number 6 was awake and crawling toward the phone. She glared at me as I went for my jacket. I untied her mouth, removed the evil leather mask, dropped it into the pillowcase. She coughed, made an unladylike sound of spitting, and stared at me. "Cop!"

"See you at Casere's, hon."

"They'll get you. This is a bunch that never forgets."

"Tell me who runs this operation and I'll say a good word for you with the DA."

"He won't listen to a dead man, honey."

I stuffed a washcloth into her mouth and opened the door for a reconnoiter. Sometimes it pays to be cautious. Down the hall, the elevator doors had just opened, and Jancey Sheridan stepped out, dressed in Levi's and a plaid cowboy jacket. Jancey's walk was insolent and cocky, and it told me he didn't know yet his operation had been hit. He carried a paper bag. I hustled back inside and counted to ten while Number 6 watched me from where

138

she sat with her back against the wall. I could hear Jancey open the door to 609.

He cursed. "Motherfuck! What the hell is—?"

The door to 609 was almost closed as I ran for the stairwell. The boots felt awkward on my feet, and the pillowcase banged against my leg. I was almost to the stairwell door when Jancey's bullet caught me high in the left shoulder. I held onto the pillowcase but dropped my rented jacket. With my right hand, I yanked the door open. Jancey was coming behind me. I knew he'd expect me to go down, so I went up. The shoulder burned like fire. At the landing where the stair made a turn, I stopped, dropped the pillowcase, and pulled my .32. I hate killing people. It leaves a bad taste in your mouth and a dark taint on your soul. I told myself not to be overconfident. The Overconfidence Express—that's the name of the train leaving this world.

The pain from the bullet made my head swirl. The stairwell door opened and Jancey Sheridan came into view. He looked down and cocked his head as he listened for steps descending. I could hear him breathing. When he looked up, I was ready for him, gun leveled.

"Drop the piece, Sheridan. The cops are on the way."

"You prick!" He fired at me in a practiced motion, the big barrel swinging up to speed me to the hereafter, and at the same time I squeezed off three shots. The noise from his big six-shooter—it looked like a .44—filled the hollow stairwell. I felt the sting of something sharp stabbing my face, and then I climbed up the stairs and out of sight.

Waiting is the hard part. I sat there for a couple of minutes, breathing hard, with warm blood oozing down my back. I felt the familiar adrenaline rush, and then a wave of dizziness. In the stairwell, I could hear only my own breathing. When nothing moved, I peeked around the concrete stair. Jancey Sheridan, Kathy's cowboy, lay sprawled against the iron safety railing.

Carrying the pillowcase, I walked to Sheridan and tested for a pulse with two fingers on his neck. I felt a faint flutter of life. In the corridor, I retrieved my jacket, picked up the paper sack, and dropped it into the pillowcase. Black spots zoomed at my eyes as I headed for the elevator. The doors whispered shut, but my attention was on the wound in my shoulder. I could not make a decision. Finally, I remembered the key ring I'd taken from the blonde. I shoved in the key and the elevator started down.

I made it out the back way, through the orange door, to the Lincoln. The time was four thirty-two and my mission was accomplished and now I needed medical attention. I unlocked the trunk. When I tossed in the pillowcase, the paper sack came open and spilled out some twenty-dollar bills. I would count them later.

I started the Lincoln.

The tapes were safe. Jancey Sheridan was dead, or close to it. The room upstairs was full of fried chicken and three hundred cassette tapes, and when Lido Enterprises found out who wrecked their operation, they would come after me.

I wanted to leave town. I wanted to cry. Instead, I headed up Pacific Coast Highway toward St. Boniface. The hospital was getting to be my second home.

11

I came awake to the sharp tang of smelling salts and the round face of Webby Smith, my pal from the Laguna Beach PD.

"Hey, Iron Man."

"Hey, Shamus. You stood me up for lunch."

Behind Webby, two faces floated. One belonged to Dr. Hunsaker, yacht captain, heart surgeon, tennis player, and Sunday socialite. The other face belonged to Agent Dorn, the Fed with the three-piece suits and the gray wolf eyes. I shivered.

"Is that tape going?" Dorn asked. "I need a statement, in case our friend here buys the farm."

"Your statement can wait, sir. This man's been through hell. He needs bed rest, a week at least."

"Goddamnit, doctor. The world's coming loose at the seams and this hot dog with the PI license knows a damn sight more than he's telling and I'm not leaving this room until I get it all on tape!"

"He's my patient, sir. I decide when he talks."

Good old Doc Hunsaker. Always around when you need him most. Girl goes overboard, here comes the doc. Get yourself shot in the fanciest hotel in Southern California, here comes the doc.

"Did you get the lead out?" My voice sounded like an echo off the moon. "Did ballistics say I shot myself?"

"Very funny, Shamus."

"This should cut the edge off that pain, Mr. Murdock." I felt something prick my arm as Hunsaker administered a hypo.

"Did you get the tapes, Webby? I left a message for you, would've waited, but I . . . got shot . . ."

"We got 'em, Shamus. A truckload."

There was a pause and I closed my eyes. Webby asked, "Tell us what went down at the Bougaineville, okay? Just hit the high spots."

I felt like trying a joke, but my mind wouldn't budge. "Did you get the lead out?"

Dorn cursed.

"Rest easy, Mr. Murdock," Hunsaker said. "The projectile entry was from the rear, leaving a hole the size of a quarter in your left thoracic region. It ripped some muscle tissue, but fortunately missed the bone. You won't be able to—"

Dorn shoved a tape recorder under my nose. "You were going to keep us informed, Murdock. You were going to play ball. Now let's have it."

"Here's how it went, Inspector, from the top. Got a hot tip on those missing coins . . . a phone call at midnight from a man with a muffled voice . . . called himself the Muffler . . . offered to sell the coins back to me at twenty cents on the dollar, so I—"

The tape recorder went away. "You're a clown, Murdock. A real clown."

"Thanks."

"Save the bullshit for the newspapers. Let me tell you what we've got. One, we have a dead man in the stairwell. Two, we have a wounded man tied up in 609, next to a shirtless foreign national who was viciously beaten. Three, next door, in 611, we have a female who claims you raped her, stole her money and her ID and six thousand dollars' worth of jewelry. Four, we have hotel clients threatening the hotel and the city of Laguna Beach with millions of dollars in civil suits. Five, we have you, the beach clown, and you can get twenty years for impeding a federal investigation."

Dead man in stairwell—that was Jancey Sheridan. "Saw a hooker," I said. "Saw some tapes, some bad guys with guns, but no sign of drugs. So go home, Mr. Fed. Go back home." I had a feeling the joke had bombed.

"Ah, bullshit." Dorn went away.

There was a long moment of whispering, and since I couldn't make it out, I concentrated on this picture inside my head—four men getting out of a long black limousine carrying violin cases, wearing dark suits, smiling hit-man smiles.

Webby stood by the bed again.

"Did they take my ankle gun, Iron Man?"

"Yeah. You know the drill. It's evidence."

"Is the cowboy dead?"

"Yeah."

"You find his piece?"

"Yeah. A .44 Colt."

The hit men opened their violin cases.

"Tote that .44 in here, Webby. Stash it with me."

143

"Why? So you can shoot yourself in the foot?"

"Stay with me, Webby."

Webby frowned as he spoke to Hunsaker. "He's scared out of his tree, doc. I know this guy."

"That's the medication," Hunsaker said. "It induces mild paranoia."

"That's some kind of medication. I didn't know Murdock would admit being scared of anything."

"Not to worry, Lieutenant. It will wear off."

I gathered my nerves together and tried again. "Hey, Iron Man?"

"Yeah?"

"Was Dorn wearing the gray three-piece or the blue pinstripe?"

Webby laughed. "Hey, good work. Joke some more."

Hunsaker went away and I counted to ten, to make sure he was gone. "Webby?"

"I'm here, Shamus."

"You sure Dorn's DEA?"

"He wears suits, doesn't he?"

"He's a prick, Webby. He's got wolf eyes."

"I'm not disagreeing. You want to tell me what went down?"

"The tape off?"

"Yeah."

"Okay." The hit men in my head went away. "My client got some dirty photos in the mail, along with a threat note asking for ten grand."

"Hennessy's widow, right?"

"Right. The photos showed her late husband in the arms of a couple of masked hookers. I advised her to call the cops. She said no. In Hennessy's desk . . . I found a slip of paper with a phone number for Lido Enterprises.

144

It was my only lead. I made a date, picked the girl up at Casere's, and drove to the Bougaineville. We had champagne. While she stripped down to her working clothes, I discovered the camera . . . behind the TV screen. I tied her up and went next door to find the tapes. The Arab kid wasn't armed, so I tied him up. While I hunted for the tapes, the door opened and a suit threw down on me. I shot the suit in self-defense, then went back for my jacket. Somewhere in there, I alerted your department. As I was heading out, like a peaceful citizen, I took a hit from behind in the shoulder. When my assailant followed, I shot him in self-defense."

"Had you ever seen any of these people before?"

"No." A white lie.

"What did you take out of there?"

"A couple of tapes."

"Where are they?"

"In my pickup." Another fib. The pickup was in for repairs.

"The Ford?"

"Yeah." I gave him the plate number and he wrote it down in his notebook.

"So it should be in the lot?"

"At the Bougaineville. I took a cab here."

Webby's look said he didn't believe me. "What was the tab for an afternoon with a hooker?"

"A grand."

Webby whistled. "Some hooker. Who paid that?"

"My client. I got that money back, of course."

"You were always tight with a nickel."

"Did you get a make on the perpetrators?"

"Yes."

"Well?"

"Goddamnit, Murdock, this is police business. Dorn will have my ass in a Federal pen if he finds out."

"Since when did you let a suit from Washington push you around?"

Webby sighed, flipped backward in his notebook. "Okay. The guy you wasted was J. L. Sheridan, of Huntington Beach. There are warrants out on him in Texas, Louisiana, Georgia, and Arkansas. They're going over his apartment now. He did three years in Huntsville for pandering. LAPD wants him for questioning in connection with a vice ring working Sunset Boulevard."

"That fits."

"Nice, huh? The suit with the leg wound is Danny D'Angelo. Danny used to work out of Vegas. We think he still has mob connections. He's served time for car theft and bunco. The cameraman with the pretty gold necklace is Tadash Farouki, who entered the country on a student visa. Tadash spent a term at a community college, then dropped out and went to work making blue movies. He's worked for Sheridan for six months."

"Who did Sheridan work for?"

"They don't know. Both D'Angelo and Farouki were paid in cash every week. Farouki ran the cameras and made the still photos. D'Angelo provided security and fried chicken. As far as they know, Sheridan was the boss."

"Any evidence of new extortion threats?"

"We found six photo packs ready to go to a messenger service."

"Famous faces?"

"Business types, a local politician, a preacher. Dorn wants you on ice, so you can't talk to the press."

Screw Dorn. "Did you quiz the bad guys about Hennessy? My guess is he died in that bed in 611."

"We quizzed 'em. They don't know nothing."

"What about the hooker?"

Webby flipped a page in his notebook.

"Last name, McGuire. First name, Alison. Went to high school in Illinois. Three years of college at Champaign-Urbana, where she majored in drama and foreign languages. Her senior year she married a professor. Two years ago, she separated from hubby and came out to California. Alison McGuire is twenty-six. She has no record." He closed his book and shook his head. "Too bad. She's the best-looking hooker I ever saw, and I've seen some hookers. What a waste."

"What's the security setup here?"

"An officer on the door, eight-hour shift. Two more patrolling."

"Not your guys?"

"No. This is Newport Beach, remember? They're Leon Book's guys."

"Where is Book, anyway?"

"He'll be along. The Bougaineville party took place in Laguna. So you got me for the first round."

"Lend me your .357, just for the night."

"Hell, no." Webby put his notebook away. "Repeat after me—'I am safe. I am safe.'"

I tried to smile. It was no use.

After Webby left, I tried watching TV. There was no one in the other bed. It was a perfect setup. Would they send a hit man? A hit lady? An orderly with a surgical blade? My eyelids felt heavy. Damn the doctor and his paranoid hypo. I kept seeing photos in my head—Kathy and Jancey Sheridan at Mrs. Mayhew's; Kathy on my sofa, wearing my shirt, reading the Hennessy folder; Sheridan walking cockily into the Bougaineville—but when I tried to put the frames together, the film spilled onto the floor. Maybe, I thought, I could get some answers from Kathy. I called her number, but the answering service said she wasn't picking up. I left another message—maybe she was gone forever—then I called Bongo Bodette.

"Hey, Sherlock. Still no luck on that El Señor R phone number. How's it hanging?"

"Can you get me a piece, Bongo?"

Bongo hesitated. "Probably from old Zeke. Anything special?"

Zeke Amado was a safecracker who could open anything that locked. He also supplied guns, ammunition, explosives, and disguises—all for a price.

"An automatic. Something bigger than a .22."

"No sweat. Where you at?"

"I'm in room 4019, at St. Boniface. There's a cop on the door. There's more patrolling outside." Bongo had an aversion to cops.

"Hell, I can send old Lucy June."

"Thanks."

"You need it quick, I reckon."

"You reckon right."

"Gotcha," Bongo said, and hung up.

I dozed. An orderly with a scraggly beard woke me. He wore hospital whites and his name tag said HICHENS. He was strong, with big biceps. I gave him five bucks to buy a six-pack. The time was ten-thirty and Bongo hadn't arrived. Hichens promised to hurry. "Twenty minutes, max."

I had to try moving, so I turned the volume down on the TV and swung out of bed. The floor was cold and my legs wobbled under me. When I opened the door, the corridor was empty and dimly lit. The cop on duty was down about halfway, talking to a nurse with dancers' legs. She wore a white uniform and one of those perky little nurse caps. When the nurse saw me standing there in my shorty hospital gown, she came around the cop, shaking her head in a tsk-tsk manner. The cop walked back with her, his hand on his revolver.

"Hey, Big Teach. How's it hanging?"

The cop was Ben Mendoza. He was in his early thirties, with coal black hair, brown eyes, and a face like a young Gilbert Roland. "Mendoza," I said. "You ever learn that diving shot?"

"I got it. I got it." We shook and he turned to the nurse. "This fellow taught me how to hit a target while playing Lone Ranger on a department chopper. Some trip, man."

Mendoza introduced the pretty nurse. Her name was Escobedo. She had big eyes and black hair and a soft, caring face. "You should be in bed, Mr. Murdock."

Mendoza and the nurse helped me back to bed. At eleven-fifteen, Hichens arrived with my six-pack of Coors in a white liquor-store bag. I invited him to have one with me. The beer lifted my spirits. The toothy people on the screen reported the state of death and chaos in the world with sincere smiles—a train accident in Oregon; another murder by the Summer Killer; an assassination attempt outside Brussels, on a huge estate owned by some rich guy.

"Some bucks for that pad," Hichens said.

"Yeah. Some bucks."

When the news was over, Hichens crushed his beer can and yawned. "I've been on twenty-four hours, man. Time to crash." He was a big hefty kid and I wanted to tell him how scared I was, wanted to ask him to stay. Sleep here, I wanted to say. Use that other bed. Just then Lucy June arrived, looking crisp and strangely starched in a rented nurse's uniform. She was carrying a paper sack and she smiled at Hichens through her thick lenses. He beamed at her.

"Hey!" he said. "You're new."

"Hey, yourself."

Hichens introduced himself and walked out. When the door closed, Lucy June came close to the bed. "Hey, Mr. Murdock. What happened?"

"I was chasing the bad guys and one of them winged me."

"Oh, you always joke about the serious stuff." She dug into the paper sack and came out with a Walther PPK/S .380 and two extra clips. "Bongo says you can owe him."

"Thanks. How much?"

"Four hundred." She looked around, "My, what a nice room."

She strolled to the window as I checked the action on the pistol. It was four years old, maybe five, but it had been well cared for. Good old Zeke. I tucked it behind my pillow.

"Okay, now you need to scoot on home."

"Aw, can't I stay? Bongo's watching trash on television. Those phony wrestlers drive me crazy."

"Sorry. There may be trouble. Bongo would never forgive me."

"Aw, Mr. Murdock—"

We were arguing when the door opened to admit Dr.

150

Hunsaker in his white jacket. He frowned when he saw Lucy June. "Nurse, I'm very weary from a long hard day. Would you be good enough to chase down to One and bring me a hot cup of Mrs. Joseph's excellent coffee?"

"Of course, doctor. Cream? Sugar?"

"You're new here, aren't you?"

"Yes, doctor."

"Just black, please. Make a note."

Lucy June left the room, and Hunsaker flashed me his best surgeon's smile while he jabbed the needle of a hypodermic into a little bottle with a red rubber cap. "Well, how's the patient?"

"Great."

The needle of the hypo glittered as it left the rubber cap. "Time for your next pain medication. Want to roll over and show me some hip?"

I held up my good hand. "No medication, doc."

Hunsaker narrowed his eyes. His head was between me and the television. I couldn't see his eyes. "But you'll need it. If we don't medicate, you'll be climbing the walls."

"No medication."

"Very well." But he didn't lower the hypo. "I'm going off the floor, but I'll make sure the nurses have their instructions." His eyes turned hard as he grabbed my right wrist. I couldn't reach the Walther, behind the pillow. The hypo descended toward my right forearm.

"You never said why you called Mrs. Mayhew last Friday."

"Your tenacity knows no bounds, Mr. Murdock."

As he jabbed the hypo down, I pulled him toward me. The needle tore through the outer layer of skin on my forearm and drove on into the mattress. I heard a light pop as the needle snapped. Hunsaker stepped back. He was breathing hard. I was dizzy.

"Damn you, sir!"

"What's in the hypo, doc? Curare?"

Hunsaker pulled a second hypo out of his pocket and I knew this was something more than painkiller. As he came close again, I heard a scuffling sound in the corridor, and someone grunted, and some glass broke. Hunsaker whirled around, the needle glinting, just as the door opened and the lights went out.

"What the bloody hell?" Hunsaker said.

There was only darkness coming from the corridor. I heard a moan. Hunsaker was asking questions, tossing them into the dark, using his command voice. "What's going on here? What's happened to the lights?"

I swung my legs to the floor. I was shaking and the hospital gown was open in back. A cool breeze chilled my backside as I stumbled to the bathroom, holding the paper sack containing the Walther.

"Murdock, what—?"

Something cut him off in mid-sentence and he cried out. In the fuzzy light from the parking lot, I saw a shadowy shape at the door and the flash of a long blade. I fired, and the .380 made a sharp cracking sound. I heard someone grunt and saw again the flicker of a blade and heard a clean whistling sound as the blade passed through the air, and then the sound of ripping.

I fired three more shots, keeping the Walther at waist-level and firing from right to left, spacing the shots and counting. The pistol cracked through the darkness, and then I heard fierce whispering, someone giving orders, someone arguing about those orders. I couldn't tell if the voices were male or female. They sounded foreign, but that could have been my imagination.

From the corridor, an alarm bell rang. The whispers were louder. I heard footsteps running away. The alarm kept clanging with long echoes, the way alarms always do when it's too late and the thieves have departed. I sat down, my back against the bathroom wall. I had a couple of rounds left, but no strength to reload. The door opened. Outside, in the corridor, a big-beam flashlight wavered and voices worked the body count.

"Christ, here's one. A nurse. Jesus!"

"Here's one. It's a cop—hell, it's Mendoza!"

"Look at the blood. Would you just look at—"

"Is that you, Harrison?"

"Yeah, who's there?"

"Sergeant Book here. Where's Mendoza?"

"He's hurt bad, Sarge."

It was Book's voice. Or maybe someone who sounded like Book. I felt paranoid. Maybe the medication was still working. Someone called my name, but I sat there without answering, holding the .380, my butt cold on the tile floor, until the lights came on and two cops charged into the room, ready to blow me away.

They dropped the Walther into a plastic evidence bag, and they helped me to the other bed. The sheets on my bed had been slashed by a very sharp blade. The foam rubber mattress showed the long cuts, three inches deep. We passed Hunsaker on the way. He was sitting with his back against the wall, holding onto his right arm, while a small pool of blood formed on the floor. A doctor in a white coat was bending over him.

"Get"—Hunsaker began—"get me a tourniquet. Prepare the OR. Call Dr. Gerson." Hunsaker glanced at me, then shifted his eyes away.

Ten feet away from Hunsaker was a body dressed in black pajamas and little Ninja boots, the kind I'd seen in the catalog in Barney Ratner's office.

"He dead?"

"Yeah."

Two orderlies helped Hunsaker out, and a uniformed cop asked me if I was hurt and I grunted. In a while, two nurses moved me to another room.

I lay in bed, staring at the ceiling, not knowing what time it was. Then Sergeant Book came in, looking like a college professor in his baggy jacket and brown summer slacks. "Hello, Murdock. TGIF, right?" He carried a paper sack.

"Is that my Coors?"

Book popped open a Coors, one of mine, and handed it over. "How many shots did you fire?"

"Five or six. It was dark."

"You always shoot in the dark, Murdock. That's the PI game, shooting in the dark." Book drank his Coors. "Whoo. Hot beer."

"What time is it?"

"After one."

"Did Webby call you?"

"Yeah. At home. Said you were worried about security."

I drank a sip of warm beer and felt a wave of nausea. "Mendoza?"

"Hurt bad. So was a nurse named Escobedo."

"Christ. How's the doc?"

"Better than they are. Used his medical know-how and

put his thumb on the right spot to stop the bleeding." Book sipped his beer. "Where'd you get the piece?"

"My secret."

"How'd you know this was going down?"

"Lucky guess."

I didn't tell him about my instinct, the one inherited from my old man, the Top Kick. The instinct was my secret, and it had pulled me through lots of battles where other guys got nailed. I didn't know how it worked—a nudge, a feeling of danger from behind—but I paid attention when it did. The Top Kick hadn't left me anything else.

"How many of them were there?" I asked.

"Three, we think, including the one you iced. Maybe four in all."

"Any ID?"

"Nothing yet. You got any more guns stashed away?"

"No. Want to loan me yours?" I rested the beer against the little side rail and held out my hand, palm up.

He stood up. "See you tomorrow. Agent Dorn wants a statement."

"Do me a favor, will you?"

"Sure, if I can."

"The doc tried to shoot me with a hypo. He seemed very intent. The stuff spilled in that other room, in the slashed-up bed. I don't think it was painkiller."

"This your famous PI hunch machine?"

"Check it out, Sergeant. Just for fun."

"You need rest, Murdock."

At 2:30 A.M., a nurse came into my new room with a paper cup full of colored pills. I said no and got ready to

155

fight her off, but she scolded me, took my temperature, and hurried away.

At dawn, I climbed out of bed. It took me a long time to get dressed. I needed food, coffee, sleep, a safe house. I had to get out of the hospital.

The cop on the door said, "Where are you going?"

"I've been discharged. No sweat."

"Hey. Okay." He walked me to the door that led to the parking lot, and we shook. "Good job last night. They say Mendoza will make it."

"Great."

I sat behind the wheel of the Lincoln wondering whether or not I would throw up. When I didn't, I cranked the engine and drove slowly out of there, toward home.

One thought kept recurring—who told them I was there, in room 4019?

It wasn't Webby. He was my pal. It wasn't Sergeant Book. He was an original straight arrow. It could have been a cop. It could have been a hospital employee. It could have been Doc Hunsaker, but then he would have known not to be in the way when they arrived with their black pajamas and their Ninja swords.

And, best of all, it could have been Agent Dorn.

It hurt to smile. It was 6:43 A.M. on a summer Saturday. Bodies were piling up. I'd been on the Hennessy case a week. I still hadn't found those gold coins.

12

Driving past the parking lot outside my house, I spotted Kathy's green Buick station wagon, so I circled around and found her behind the wheel, staring out at the beach. I rapped on the window, startling her. She had circles under her eyes and her blue blouse was rumpled. She opened the door and stepped out, brushing a strand of hair away from her face.

"What happened?" She indicated my left arm in the hospital sling.

"Friend of yours shot me."

"It's too early to joke." She gave me a half smile.

"Jancey Sheridan."

The smile froze and her eyes widened. She sank back against the car. "Oh, God. Oh, dear God!"

"Well, you said he was a crook."

She nodded dully, then coughed. "What happened . . . to Jancey?"

"I killed him."

She pushed away from the car and came close and put her arms around me. For a moment, we stood there, not talking, just holding each other. Above us, a hungry gull circled and screamed.

"Can we go upstairs? I have something to tell you."

"We can't stay, Kathy. I came by for some clothes and stuff."

There was alarm in her voice. "Where are you going?"

"A motel I know."

"A motel? Why?"

"It's not safe here."

Kathy stared around at the deserted beach, where nothing stirred. "Not safe? It's so peaceful here."

"They came for me last night, in the hospital."

"Who?"

"Jancey's crowd."

She gulped, then tried to look brave. "I'll come with you."

"You sure?"

She took my good arm. "Yes. Very."

In my place, Kathy packed us a lunch from my fridge while I stuffed underwear and socks and a clean shirt into my olive drab duffle. We made a first trip down to the Lincoln and I came back for my .357, the Colt Diamondback, the AR-15, a shotgun, and some ammo. I rolled the fridge out from the wall and pulled out the emergency fund, two thousand dollars. The time was seven-oh-five.

Then, with Kathy following in her Buick, I headed up Coast Highway to the Dorado Motel in Huntington Beach. I wanted two rooms, but Kathy said she wanted to be close. We registered as Mr. and Mrs. Whitlington. The room had twin beds.

She gave me arnica for my shoulder. While she took a shower, I went out for coffee and Danish and a six-pack at the 7-Eleven. When I came back, she was wearing a close-fitting robe and she had a towel around her wet hair. The motel room was filled with the taut tension of the unexplained. While we ate, I told her about Jancey and the Bougaineville and the action at the hospital.

"Terrible."

"Okay, Kathy. That's my story. Why are you here? Why can't you go home?"

"They were waiting for me, this morning, when I flew in."

"Flew in from where?"

"Colorado."

"Who was waiting?"

"Some people I know. I recognized the cars and I came straight here to you." She gave me a smile. "Lovely coffee. It antidotes the arnica, so you should be drinking tea."

"I'll take my chances with the coffee. And I'm still waiting." She turned away from me without answering and stared at the wall. Then she set the coffee cup down and opened her suitcase, an expensive leather job by Gucci. She took out a leather-bound book and handed it to me. It was two inches thick and heavy. The pages were letter-size. I waited before opening it. When Kathy finally spoke, her voice was thick with emotion. "I'm a hooker, Matt. A lady of the night. I work for Mrs. Mayhew. Or did. This journal contains records that go back ten years. I've got names, dates, places, fees paid for services rendered."

"Jesus Christ." I felt like an ox in a slaughterhouse. "Mrs. Mayhew! Jesus H. Christ!"

"I know and I'm sorry. Will you help me?"

I was dazed, dizzy, hurt. There was a bittersweet taste in my mouth. "Help you how?"

"She owes me two hundred thousand dollars . . . in commissions. I came back for the money."

"From Colorado."

"Yes. Colorado Springs. My daughter's there. She was in a car accident Thursday. She needs some very expensive care." Tears rolled down Kathy's cheeks.

"This is the daughter from the—?"

"Yes. The rape. I gave her up for adoption."

"You poor kid." I put my good arm around her and she leaned into me. For a while, there was only the sound of her quiet sobbing. Then she went into the bathroom and washed her face. When she came out, the story continued.

"My daughter's name is Lisa and she's seventeen, which is the same age I was when I gave her away."

"Does she know who you are?"

"Well, almost. She thinks I'm an aunt, the younger sister of her mother, who supposedly died in childbirth. We've had good talks. Lisa wants to live with me, but I'd die if she found out about my life. You can understand that. I've been saving money, hoping to say good-bye to Angela Mayhew and Lido Enterprises, but Angela needs me for the operation, for keeping things running smoothly, so she held out on me, calling it cash flow problems. You were right. When I left you the other night, I wasn't planning on coming back. Then Lisa had her accident, and the sixty thousand in the kitty wasn't nearly enough, so I came back for what's mine. I kept good records . . . in that book." Her voice was determined. "For an occasion just like this."

"Can't the parents help with Lisa?"

"He's out of work, so his insurance has lapsed. It's up to me."

"What's your plan on the money?"

Kathy tapped the book with her index finger. "I sent some Xeroxed pages to Angela Mayhew, offering to sell my silence. So she sent those people to watch my house."

I thought of the Ninjas at the hospital. "One good thing."

"What?"

"At least she took you seriously."

Kathy shivered. "Yes."

"If you sell her the book, you're dead. No more insurance policy. If you try to sell silence, she'll just laugh."

"What can I do?"

I shook my head. "Let me think about it. I'm beat. We can't do much until night."

"Night? That's hours away!"

"Yeah. But I'm beat anyway."

Kathy stood up and looked down at me, and I had the feeling she had just dumped her problem in my lap. How long had she been thinking of doing just that?

"I'd like a beer. You?"

"Too early for me," I said. And then: "Oops. Changed my mind."

She brought the beers to the bed. We lay on separate beds, propped up on motel pillows, while she told her story.

"Remember Oreo cookies?"

"Sure. Chocolate on the outside. Sugary white goo on the inside."

"Well, I was an Oreo junkie and a book freak. I hated the world and read all the time—books, true confession

161

magazines—and when I read, I ate Oreo cookies. I used to lick the white stuff off first, and then suck the cookies while I read. I drove my mom crazy, but my dad understood. He was an artist. He encouraged my writing. My favorite story was 'Fat Cinderella.'"

"Good title, 'Fat Cinderella.'"

"Fat Cinderella pines for the big football jock, the prince of the high school, but he won't look at her. He snickers at her behind her back. So she signs up with Weight Watchers, loses seventy pounds, gets real sexy, and steals the heart of the prince away. Only I couldn't make the transfer from the world of my imagination to the real world. Writing let me escape and gave me control. When I went back to the real world, however, the kids still made jokes about my flab.

"All that changed when I was seventeen. My legs got longer. My face lost its baby fat. I worked in a summer camp for rich kids near Gunnison, took off thirty pounds, and came home tanned and sleek. Boys who had ignored me three months before started asking me out. I was overwhelmed. I was outclassed. Other girls knew how to handle the male animal. Not me. On a date after a football game a boy named Freddy Hedren raped me in the front seat of his pickup and by Christmas I knew I was pregnant."

Kathy paused to sip some beer. "It was pretty awful. He tore my panties and pulled my hair. The bruises stayed on my legs for a month. I went limp and closed my eyes and stopped fighting. It was over very fast. At school, I wore baggy sweaters, to hide the baby growing inside me. I had to drop out of school. I wanted an abortion, but Daddy convinced me to have the baby, a little girl. I cried buckets when I gave her up for adoption.

162

And that day I started building my wall. No one, I swore, would ever hurt me again. No one would touch me. I would be above it all."

"I've tried that myself." I reached out to touch her hand and she gave me a brief smile.

There was silence in the room. Outside, a single siren moaned up Coast Highway. Kathy went back to her story.

"In college at CU I had a job clerking in the college bookstore. I loved it there, all those books. But the pay was lousy, so I worked the four-to-eleven shift serving cocktails at the Boulder Lodge. I'd finish work and run through the crystal-cold nights to the campus. I had a room to myself, crammed with books and papers and pencils. I wrote all night, read everything I got my hands on. Joyce. Yeats. Kafka. Proust. Eliot. Since I didn't have love to distract me, I made all A's. The profs said I was a cinch for a graduate fellowship. When I was a junior, I sold the Fourth of July piece. The next year, I sold a version of 'Fat Cinderella' to a women's magazine. My wall was up and working. I was in heaven."

"What about men?"

"Um. Only double dates. No kissing. No petting. Word got around Fraternity Row and they left me alone. I'm sure they thought I was gay. I honestly didn't miss men. I lived for my work. And there was Arlene."

"Your roommate. The one who got you the job in L.A."

"You do have a memory, don't you?" Kathy studied me a minute before going on. "I was a senior. She was a graduate student in drama. I'll never forget the way she'd walk into a seminar in Yeats or Browning, wearing heels and a dress. In the winter she'd wear her sable. She was tall, flashy, quick-witted. She made A's without working too hard. She had a personality like Susan Hayward and she dated older men, with big cars and lots of money. One day Arlene invited me for coffee and we exchanged life stories. We had Colorado in common. We both liked literature, novels, poetry. Arlene made me laugh. She also made me envious. She had a house in the fanciest section of Boulder, a gorgeous four-bedroom home with a fireplace and a view and a built-in steam bath. When her roommate moved out to get married, Arlene invited me to move in. I knew my salary as a cocktail waitress wouldn't cover it. 'No problem,' Arlene said. 'You've been around. Let me introduce you to some benevolent benefactors.' She was smiling. I knew what she meant. Men. I said no. We argued. I told her about my rape, the pregnancy. She'd been raped when she was fifteen. Her confession made us both cry. We ended up in the steam bath, very drunk, very naked. You can guess what happened when she started kissing my tears away and I was liking it a lot. Oh, I knew what lesbians were, in theory at least. I'd read Anaïs Nin and Gloria Steinem. I'd had my personal fling with the ideology of feminism. But that snowy night with Arlene I found something I needed more. She offered. I took."

Kathy was quiet for a moment. The mood in the room was fragile, like thin glass. She shifted her weight slightly on the bed.

"Loneliness drove me to Arlene. But it was curiosity, too. How could she sell herself? How could she allow men to do that to her? Her answer was simple. 'Honey,' she said. 'It's not me they're fucking. It's their mother or daughter, sometimes their sister. For years, they spy on their sister undressing, going crazy for her, and later on when they grow up and the itch is half buried, they find me and I sell them their substitute fix.' It sounded logical

164

but simplistic, but she was my only friend. I moved in with Arlene, and in ten days she'd introduced me to a rancher and a banker and two corporation higher-ups from Denver. On my first trick, I made a hundred dollars for thirty seconds of quick sex and forty-five minutes of listening to the rancher tell me how guilty he felt lusting after his daughter, a Pi Phi on campus. I knew the girl. She was a dopehead, a dumb one who'd already had an abortion. And her daddy thought she lit the sun in the morning. Arlene had been right. It was the substitution game.

"That summer Arlene and I took a trip to Vegas. We drove her new Chrysler convertible, a gift from an admirer. We turned a few tricks, but it was spooky, because the town was organized into Mob sectors. Two different pimps tried to recruit us. The money was good, two hundred a trick, sometimes three. Arlene decided to stay. But I wanted to finish my M.A. degree, so I went back without her. I wrote in my journal: 'Arlene goes for the big time.'

"Back at school, I got the lonelies. I lived in the pretty house, handled the clients. I made money, but I was unhappy. A nice old rancher in his fifties proposed to me. I spent Christmas in New York with my younger brother, who was being shipped out to the Persian Gulf. Then I spent New Year's with Arlene in Palm Springs. She had a new friend—Mrs. Landis Mayhew."

Pieces kept falling into place.

"What year was this?"

"Nineteen seventy-seven. Mrs. Mayhew was her charming self. There were other girls there and we sort of paired off with the men. I remember a senator, a mayor from a very large city, an army general, and a corporation executive. I made a special friend there. His name was Gunther. He was a European, very bright, with a nice sense of humor. Everyone knew him. No one knew exactly what he did."

"I think I'm jealous."

Kathy stretched her arms over her head. "Gunther owned the house in Palm Springs. He was in his early fifties then. He swam every day to stay in shape. He knew literature, films, geography, music. When we'd finish making love, he'd go into the bathroom and read. There were books everywhere. We discussed my yen for writing and he took my novel manuscript with him when he left. He never pressured me about sex. He gave me a diamond bracelet, four Canadian Maple Leafs, and an American Express Card with a twenty-thousand-dollar limit. He still pays the Amex bill. I still have those Maple Leafs. An hour after Gunther was gone, Mrs. Mayhew offered us jobs, complete with a pension plan, sick pay, and a beach house in Malibu. We worked out of Malibu for five years. Then Arlene got married and Mrs. Mayhew moved to Newport Beach, to become queen of Balboa Peninsula. I came along as a trainer."

"Did you see Gunther again?"

"I used to see him every three or four months. He'd come to the States, or I would fly to Europe."

"Did you meet in Palm Springs?"

"We met mostly in New York, sometimes in Vegas. Gunther loves the theater."

"So did you, right?"

"Don't stay jealous, okay? Gunther could have any woman he chose. He gave me presents. He never lied to me. If he couldn't tell the truth, he'd shake his head and look sad."

"Tell me about the money Mrs. Mayhew owes you."

"As trainer, I got five percent of every trick."

"What was the girl's cut?"

"Forty per cent. The rest went for overhead and expenses."

"How does old Landis figure in?"

"She keeps him around for laughs. He's fallen in love with half a dozen girls in the last five years. He's her court jester."

"Did he fall for you?"

"I'd call it a schoolboy crush. Very unbecoming in an older man. Poor Landis."

"What happened to Hennessy?"

Kathy paused for a long moment. "He had a heart attack in bed. Jancey's people drove him to Irvine. They were supposed to park him near his home, but they got confused and went to Ron's."

I thought of Tadash and Danny D'Angelo. "Good help is hard to find."

"It's not funny, Matt."

"Who was with Hennessy when he died? Which girl?"

"Sally Anne."

"Jesus. I should have known."

"She was hysterical the night it happened, then very depressed. She'd never even been to a funeral. The only dead people she'd seen were on TV. When we found out she'd gone overboard on your boat, we hurried right over. Angela was furious with her."

"Hunsaker called you, didn't he?"

Kathy nodded. "The doctor was very agitated. He'd been . . . intimate with Sally Anne. Several times. He's our staff physician. He makes sure the girls take care of themselves."

"I think Hunsaker tried to ice me last night. With a hypo."

"He has a lot to lose."

"Is he in the book?"

"Yes."

"So," I said, letting out a long breath, "you know Tommy Talbot. You know Barney Ratner. You know Hunsaker. Who else do you know?"

She reached across from her bed to touch me. "Please, Matt. Don't. I haven't turned a trick in four years."

I went to the bathroom to wash my face and stare at myself in the mirror. My beard had a new tuft of gray. My eyes looked like they'd been in a Vietnamese prison camp. I came back to my bed, feeling used.

"What was that scene at Mrs. Mayhew's party all about? You remember, the one where I took some hits from Jancey?"

"Mrs. Mayhew wanted to check your reflexes, so she told Jancey to stop by. Landis hates Jancey. She knew he'd make a fool of himself."

"Why would Landis hate Jancey? His cowboy clothes?"

"I thought you'd guessed. Jancey was Mrs. Mayhew's chief stud. It drove Landis crazy. He's very possessive and believes firmly in the double standard for married couples."

I grunted. I had missed it. Maybe I was getting too old for this line of work. "What was all that shit about hiring me at three grand a week?"

"She was serious about that. Coming back from the hospital, she started planning her approach. You have the same last name as her mentor, Cassie Murdoc."

"I thought that was all bullshit."

"Angela has some odd ways. But she reads people

faster than anyone I've known. Except Gunther." Kathy drained her beer and set the can down.

"How come you stuck around?"

"Habit, I suppose. You get into ruts. The money was good, more than I could make in the real world. I had fun running Chez Lido. I was good at the training. I didn't have to turn tricks."

I thought of Bongo's list. "Are there other businesses like Chez Lido?"

"Half a dozen."

"For laundering money, right? The johns pay in cash. You run it through fake businesses."

"Chez Lido's a real business. Last year we broke even."

"Who set this up? How extensive is it?"

"No one knows how extensive, but Gunther runs things, the whole show. It was his idea, his conception, his organizational structure. He flies over, picks up his cash, and stashes it in Zurich on his return trip. He set Mrs. Mayhew up after he met her in Paris in the sixties. I was in Zurich with him a couple of times. He'd have a suitcase full of money, and I'd have to stay at the hotel while he took it to the bank."

"How many other operations are there?"

"Vegas. The Bay Area. Los Angeles. Reno. Phoenix. Dallas. Houston. Those are the ones I know about."

"We should fly to Europe and take Gunther to a bank and have him make a withdrawal."

"You couldn't get to him. No one can." Kathy looked at me. "Maybe you saw it on the news. Someone bombed his estate, outside Brussels."

"Was that Gunther?"

"Yes. Friday night."

"Okay, with all the trips to Zurich, how do you know Mrs. Mayhew has money?"

"The safe is crammed. Dollars. Yen. Swiss francs. She grew up dirt poor. She believes in Howard Ruff, about keeping a large amount of money around."

"We'll hit the safe."

"Can you do that?"

"No. But I know someone who can."

"What if she's there?"

"Move over, Mrs. Mayhew."

"Latrice can shoot, Matt. I've seen her. And she has more people around like . . . Jancey."

"Move over, Latrice. Move over, goons."

"You mean it, don't you?"

I thought of the hospital and that made me angry all over again. "I owe them some hits."

13

Kathy finished her story before noon, and since neither of us had slept much Friday night, we took a siesta. When we woke, it was three. Kathy helped me with a sponge bath, and then I dressed and drove her Buick wagon to a phone booth four blocks away and made three phone calls. The first one was to Webby Smith at the Laguna Beach PD.

"Hey, Shamus," Webby said as he came on the line. "I was worried."

"Because I left the hospital?"

"Nah. I knew you'd split. Because someone shot up your place on the pier. When the reports came in, I thought you'd been wasted."

I broke out into a sweat. "How bad?"

"You've got bullet holes in everything you own. The front door won't close. There isn't a window left in the place, or a mirror. Your answer machine is totaled. Ditto, the stereo and TV. The good news is an alert citizen called the police and they nabbed one of the shooters."

"Anyone I know?"

"His name's Boyd Hawley. Know him?"

"A biker, dirty hair, a black T-shirt and a beer gut?"

"That's him. Well, poor old Boyd says he owes you for last summer at the Blue Beat, when you hit him with a two-by-four on his blind side."

"It was a chair, and Boyd came at me with biker chains and a Rambo knife."

"I remember the knife. Anyway, Leon's got Boyd on ice, but his two biker pals are on the loose."

"What kind of hardware?"

"Boyd had a Uzi in his bike bag. No word yet from Ballistics on the rest."

"Who were they working for?"

"Boyd didn't know. The way his story goes, some biker he never saw before offered him two bills to shoot up your place. When he found out it was you, he accepted."

"That biker got away, right?"

"Right."

"What time did this happen?"

"Seven-thirty, or a couple minutes after. What time did you leave there?"

"About seven."

"Good timing."

"Thanks."

"I took a look around the hotel parking lot for your Ford pickup. Couldn't find it."

"Did you write up a report on it?"

"Not yet. You were driving some other vehicle, weren't you?"

"Yeah."

"Because you didn't want me seeing what you took out of the Bougaineville."

"You can see it anytime. I didn't want Dorn seeing it."

"You're just envious of his wardrobe fund."

"I knew guys like Dorn in Vietnam. They'd come out from Washington in their Abercrombie and Fitch safari clothes and drink beer in air-conditioned splendor while they tossed geopolitics at us."

"I hear revenge in your tone, Shamus."

"How would you feel if they shot up your house?"

"I'm not arguing. Just stay cool, okay? Speaking as a friend, I can offer this sage advice."

"Speaking as a police officer, what about a make on the Ninja from the hospital?"

"Now that," Webby said, "is interesting." Papers rustled and the phone went clunk on a table. I heard Webby curse. "Here it is. His name was Clarence Dayton. Born in Atlanta. Clarence had warrants on him in New York, New Jersey, North Carolina, and Georgia, mostly armed robbery and assault. He's wanted for questioning in two bombings of prominent citizens back East. No record of military service. His age at time of death was thirty-nine. His current address is Las Vegas, a nice touch. And, get this, Interpol says Clarence spent some time at Kwan Doc."

"Where he learned to be a Ninja."

"Right."

Kwan Doc was a secret martial arts training facility. It started in Tibet, then moved to North Korea.

"Any trace on the others?"

"We think one was wounded. There was a blood trail down the stairs. They got in wearing hospital greens. Once inside, they trimmed down to black pajamas and swords. If it's any consolation, I wish I'd listened to you, Murdock. I should have insisted on more protection . . . even if it wasn't my town."

"Thanks. How's Mendoza? How's that nurse?"

"They'll make it. We almost lost Mendoza."

"What about that stuff Hunsaker wanted to shoot me with?"

"Leon Book's lab people are supposed to be working on it."

"And where did you last see Agent Dorn?"

"At your place. Around nine."

"He went through my place?"

"Yeah. Along with the lab guys and forty other cops."

"Looking spiffy, I'll bet."

"Yeah. Looking spiffy."

I had an idea. "How would it be if I gave you a lead on some illicit drugs? Could you pass it to Dorn?"

"Sure. Hit me."

"I'll call back."

"Goddamn. When?"

"Seven. Seven-thirty."

"Where are you now?"

"I'm in Santa Barbara," I lied, "and heading north."

"Keep going, okay?"

"I'll call, Iron Man. Hang loose."

"You're up to something. I can hear it in—"

After talking to Webby, I took the time to make some notes about the chain of events. I do that when the world speeds by like a bullet train. Sometimes making notes helps to line up your ducks before you shoot.

My second phone call was to Slavick's Garage. They were just closing and the pickup was ready. I asked them to leave it parked in front. I had a spare set of keys. They could bill me for it.

My third phone call was to Bongo Bodette.

"Hey, Sherlock. Thanks for sending Lucy June back. You okay?"

"Yeah. That Walther saved my butt."

"It ain't registered, if that's what you mean."

"Great. Listen, the reason I'm calling . . . you mad at anyone? Someone you can't get at?"

Bongo thought a minute. "Besides the president and the Pentagon and the Fed and the IMF and the Club of Rome?"

"Yeah. Someone local. Someone you'd like to drop a bulldozer on."

"Herman Helguera," Bongo said. "He deals coke out of a rock house in Santa Ana. Bastard owes me two grand for some financial work. What are you planning?"

"Are you resigned to getting your revenge while you kiss the money good-bye?"

There was a short pause. "Here's the address."

I wrote it down. "Good. Could you have Zeke Amado give me a call?" I gave Bongo the number of the Dorado Motel.

After hanging up, I left Kathy's wagon in a crowded parking lot near Coast Highway and walked back to the motel through the August heat. Kathy, in shorts and a cutoff T-shirt, was watching television. She had curled her hair. Her bare legs looked pretty. When I told her about the shooting at my place, her eyes got wet and she cried again. Zeke Amado called at four-thirty and we made a date for eight at Mrs. Mayhew's on Channel Road.

Over hamburgers and French fries, Kathy and I argued about her going along.

"I know the house, damnit, and it's my money you're going after. I can shoot. I'd love to shoot her."

"Too dangerous. I want to be in and out of there in fifteen minutes. Also, I don't want you spotted. That's why I moved your wagon."

"So I'm trapped here?" She indicated our room. "Trapped in a motel in Huntington Beach?"

"For a while."

"Please, Matt. Let me go along."

"You stay put."

"What about the alarms? Angela has the house wired like a bank."

"Zeke can handle the alarms."

"What if you don't come back?"

"Don't say dumb things, okay?"

At seven, I left Kathy fuming at the motel and drove the Lincoln to a phone booth and called Webby Smith. I told him about Helguera's rock house in Santa Ana. "It's the dope headquarters for Orange County."

"Dorn will pee in his pants."

"Don't tell him you got it from me, okay?"

"I was at the Newport Beach station an hour ago. He's not looking as spiffy. He's got two cars out hunting for you alone."

"The Plymouth or the Ford?"

"The Plymouth."

"Thanks, Webby. After tonight, they're gonna put you on that task force."

"Goddamn, I've died and gone to cop's heaven."

I hung up and headed south. Traffic was medium on Coast Highway, and by seven forty-five I had checked the neighborhood on Balboa and Channel and Ocean and was parked down the street from Mrs. Mayhew's. There were lights burning on all three floors, but I didn't see anyone moving around inside. Zeke Amado arrived at seven-fifty in his van with EASY ROOTER written on the side in blue letters. He pulled into the driveway and got out, wearing his blue Easy Rooter uniform. Zeke looks like a college professor. He's thin, with narrow stooped shoulders and pale blue eyes that fool you by appearing vague. The vague look is a disguise enhanced by wire-framed glasses. Zeke, who's a history buff, calls them his "Trotsky glasses." He has sensitive hands with long fingers that can take hold of a safe dial like it's a human heart. Zeke is ten years younger than I am, but still acts like my dad.

"Hello, Matthew. My, this is upscale."

"Glad you could help me out, Zeke."

He surveyed the house over my shoulder. "This one will be five hundred, Matthew. Plus my usual ten percent."

Zeke's had his share of dry holes. I grinned and handed him five hundred dollars. Then I sat in his van while he knocked out the alarms. In three minutes, he was back, smiling a thin smile. We entered the house through a side door in the garage, which led to a laundry room I hadn't seen on my Sunday tour. I admired his speed with lock picks. I'm fast, but Zeke is a wizard. Zeke went to work on the floor safe in the library while I checked out the house.

Without the fancy society guests, Mrs. Mayhew's house echoed with emptiness. If you closed your eyes, you could hear gay laughter, the clink of Waterford, all those witty barbs. It looked like the whole crowd had left in the middle of one of Mrs. Mayhew's parties. The champagne glasses were lined up along the bar. Ashtrays smelled of tobacco. In one corner, I found a mirror and three lines of coke and a cute little straw. On one table sat three trays of wilted canapés.

My .357 out and ready, the AR-15 slung on my right shoulder, I checked the rooms. The house was empty. All the beds were made. No one was home at Mayhew Castle. In the master bedroom, I went quickly through Mrs. Mayhew's wardrobe—white and gold, white and gold. There were some pale blue dresses at the back of the walk-in closet, leftovers from another era. The bathroom fixtures were gold. The television was wired for eighty-seven channels. The sheets were sleek silk, a pale gold color.

Behind the blue dresses, I found a second safe. The door stood ajar, and except for a handwritten note, the safe was empty. The note consisted of one word, printed in gold ink on white paper. The one word was "Fool." I wanted to take thirty minutes and bust up her place, an eye for an eye, the way she'd busted mine. I felt angry and vengeful, but I couldn't afford waking up the neighborhood.

I found Zeke at the desk in the library, thumbing through a book. The floor safe was open and there was a small pile of stock certificates on the rosewood desk. Zeke closed the book and stood up.

"Not a thing in the safe, Matthew. These were tucked away in a fake electric outlet."

"Are they worth anything?"

"This is out of my area of expertise. You'll have to ask Bongo."

"What about the rest of the house?"

"There's china, quite a good collection of Rosenthal, but it would take a truck to transport. There's Waterford, but I hear the resale market's glutted. I didn't find any cash anywhere. Sorry."

"Thanks for trying. What were you reading?"

"Volume Five of Jung's collected works. Know him?"

"Isn't he the guy who thinks trees and light poles are phallic symbols?"

Zeke chuckled. "That's Freud, Matthew. Jung was far more subtle, far more accurate."

I acknowledged Zeke's superior intellect and took a last look around. How many tricks had been turned to build this house and deck it out for Newport Beach society?

Zeke put his gear back into his leather satchel and we walked out. "Should we lock up or leave it for the Vandals and the Huns?"

"Leave it."

"This is a five-million-dollar home, Matthew."

"Had to cost seven million to build."

"That much? I found the owner's taste lacking."

"Yeah."

"You should read some Jung, Matthew. It would aid you in your line of work and help you to read people with alacrity. For example, he has this handy archetype theory. The male archetype is the animus. The female is the anima. A rough translation is soulmate. The theory is, a woman is attracted to a man because he is her animus. There are four levels of the animus, four levels of the anima. The most interesting for me is the second level of the anima, represented by Helen of Troy. She is Romance, Art, Sex—"

We were outside. I closed the gate. Zeke got back to business.

"Should we reset the alarms?"

"Nah. Forget it."

He opened the door to his van. "There's more. According to Jung, a man is attracted to a woman because she is his anima."

"You believe that shit, Zeke?"

"Oh, yes. It makes lots of sense . . . if you're interested in explaining the twists and turns of the human psyche. Have you seen *The Blue Angel*?"

My mind was on action. "How soon can you get me some plastique explosive, four or five timers, a stun gun, and a stepladder?"

Zeke thought a minute. He doesn't like being interrupted when he's philosophizing. "A day. Two. When do you need it?"

"Midnight."

"Eight hundred, Matthew."

I handed him the money. "Just get it, okay."

"Will you need my services? I'd love a caper. August has been exceedingly dull."

"If I do, I'll let you know."

We shook hands and I headed for the Lincoln and Zeke drove off. On my way back to the motel, I turned the Lincoln in at the rental office at John Wayne Airport. The Plymouth started right away. Checking for cops, I took Newport Boulevard inland to Slavick's Garage. The Ford was parked out front. It took a couple of minutes to transfer some gear, and then I went back up Coast Highway to the motel.

Kathy was waiting. She still wore the shorts and the cut-off T-shirt. In her hand she clutched my Colt Diamondback. When I came in, she hugged me mightily, then put her mouth up for a kiss.

She held onto me. "I'm so glad to see you, Matt. I was so worried."

"The house was empty. The money was gone."

She stepped away in disappointment. "Everything?"

"Some stock certificates. They could be tough to negotiate." I handed them over and opened a beer.

Kathy stood in the center of the room, studying the stock certificates. Her face was hard; her eyes were narrowed. "You checked both safes?"

"Yeah. And the fake electrical outlets. Zeke's good. He doesn't miss much."

Kathy slumped down in a chair to rest her chin in her palms. "I feel terrible."

I opened a beer and climbed onto the bed. After a couple of sips, I said, "I have one more idea."

"What?"

"Think you could show me Gunther's house? In Palm Springs?"

"Of course!" She brightened. "She might go there. But she knows I know."

"Yeah. But she doesn't know you told me. So far, she doesn't know you're in town."

Kathy shivered and hugged herself. "God, I'm afraid."

"Two hours of driving and we'll know. How big is it?"

"A dozen rooms. A separate house for the servants. When I was there last, a couple of years ago, the electric gate wasn't working and Gunther was grumbling about the expense of keeping up the closed-circuit security setup. There's a fence and probably guards. How would we get in?"

"I went over a fence once using a stepladder. It's not very dashing, but it works."

"Where will you get a stepladder at this time of night?"

"Same place I'm getting some other stuff."

"You really want to do this?"

"It's our only shot. Why don't you get a paper and pencil and draw me a diagram of the house and grounds."

"What will you do?"

"Rest. Think. Maybe watch a little television."

"Are you really this calm?"

I grinned. "No."

She went to work on her diagram.

I drank beer and watched the pretty people on the TV screen. I was very tired and I felt dirty and I couldn't have a real shower because of the bandage on the shoulder wound.

After a few moments, Kathy looked up. "You're not leaving me behind again?"

"No."

"Good." She kept on drawing. "Did I tell you about the secret door?"

"What secret door?"

"There's a secret door in the master bedroom. A bookshelf swings open and there's a passage to the next room."

"Where you stayed?"

She nodded and went back to her drawing. I was liking Gunther less and less. It would be a pleasure to invade his house, whether Mrs. Mayhew was there or not.

At ten, the Channel 5 news had a rousing five minutes on a big police raid on a rock house in central Santa Ana. There were some award-winning action shots of officers in bulletproof vests converging on a dark structure in the center of the screen. The reporter on the scene had statements from Leon Book and Webby Smith and a SWAT commander from Santa Ana named Harrigan. I'd taught Harrigan to shoot, back when I was an instructor at the local academy.

There was no sign of Agent Dorn.

14

By midnight, I had the plastique and the timers and
the stepladder and the police stun gun from Zeke, and by
4 A.M., Kathy and I were heading east on the Riverside
Freeway, toward the desert and Palm Springs. There was
a moon waning behind us. The desert night was cool, and
we kept the windows up and the radio tuned to KNX.
The Ford hummed along. Kathy sat on her side, her feet
curled under her. She wore khaki slacks and a blue work
shirt under a light sweater and New Balance running
shoes.

We went over the plan three times, and then I asked
questions so I could tie up more loose ends.

"Does Mrs. Mayhew know about Colorado?"

"No. Arlene knows. And you. No one else."

"Not Gunther?"

"Not even Gunther. I told him I was from Kansas City.
Daddy died six years ago, and my mother married a fast-

food franchisee and moved to Texas. We haven't communicated since Daddy's funeral."

"Who came up with the number system, and the fake names for the johns?"

"Mrs. Mayhew claims credit for that. I think it was Gunther's idea."

"Did you have a number?"

"Um. Everyone did."

"What was it?"

"I'd like to leave that behind, Matt."

"Okay."

We drove awhile in silence before she told me. "Twelve," she said. "I was Number Twelve."

"And Sally Anne?"

"Number Eighteen."

"Where did she go, anyway?"

"Vegas. She was rotated."

"Is she okay?"

"Oh, sure. I miss her."

"Rotated. That's an ugly word."

"Yes. But very accurate."

I drove along awhile without talking. "Okay. So Mrs. Mayhew heard my last name and made a mystical connection between me and her role model."

"Yes."

"Was she a madame, too? Cassie Murdoc?"

"More like a courtesan, according to Angela. You can't separate the myth from the reality, but men supposedly traveled from as far as Berlin and Paris to spend a glorious weekend with Cassie."

"Okay. So Mrs. Mayhew reads my tea leaves and offers me a job. And were you part of the deal?"

"At first. She knew there was chemistry between us, so she sent me in to check you out."

"Like a spy."

"If you like."

"Mata Hari."

"The second time, I came on my own."

"Thanks. Makes an aging detective feel attractive."

"I liked you right away. That should have been obvious. When we kissed on the pier, I felt something I hadn't felt in a long, long time. That frightened me. I do have my walls, after all."

"And then you saw the Hennessy file."

"Yes. But by then, things were already coming apart. When we heard about poor Mr. Hennessy, Angela went straight to Dr. Hunsaker, and he went straight to his son, the county coroner, and they did something to stop the investigation. Angela brought all the girls together and gave a speech about business as usual and another record year on the balance sheet and the bonuses that would result. But she didn't count on Sally Anne jumping overboard."

"How does Dorn fit in?"

"I'm not sure. I have a feeling Gunther sent him."

"Had you known him before?"

"No. He's new. There was another man—a red-haired man—who used to come around every couple of months. He was rough with the girls, but Mrs. Mayhew was afraid of him, so he got pretty much what he wanted."

"What do these guys do?"

"Snoop around. Ask questions. Smile phony smiles."

"Which girl did Dorn like?"

"No one, that I know of. He and Latrice were kind of thick."

"Where did she come from?"

"Angela brought her back from one of her trips. A couple of years ago. She gives me the creeps. She does karate and Tai Chi every single day. She wants to be Bruce Lee's reincarnation."

"Why didn't you get out?"

"You already asked that. I'd wanted out for a year. But she owed me money, and then the monkey business with the coroner really convinced me. I just didn't figure on Lisa getting hurt."

"Did you know about the Jancey Sheridan shake-down?"

"No. I knew he had something going when he kept flashing these huge rolls of cash around. I had no idea he would try to blackmail our . . . clients. Of course, Jancey despised Angela. And he underestimated her. She'd have thanked you for killing him."

"So she didn't know about the shakedown either?"

"I'm sure she didn't. She kept films for insurance. Blackmail hurts business."

We came into Palm Springs off Interstate 10 onto Highway 111 while it was still dark. I figured we had thirty minutes, maybe forty, before first light. Gunther's house was south of town, in among some low hills near an Indian reservation. Kathy found the street on the second pass, using the big five-cell flashlight.

"How far is it?"

"About seven miles, I think. Maybe eight."

It was city road for a mile or so, then county road, then we saw a sign in the headlights saying county mainte-nance ended and the road got bumpy and we hit our first chuckhole. "Gunther's not keeping the place up."

"Maybe she's not here, Matt."

"Maybe so."

"What will we do then?"

"Go home broke."

"She'll be here. I know she will."

I kept the Ford at a steady fifteen miles per hour as we began to climb slowly and the road narrowed. We saw two signs that said PRIVATE ROAD and one that said FOR SALE. It was still dark outside and I didn't want to alert them with headlights coming over a hill, so I drove using only the parking lights and every tenth of a mile I got out and ran ahead until I was sure we weren't on top of the place. The fifth time I ran ahead I spotted lights and saw the building, a big dude on a low hill about a quarter of a mile ahead. The air still held an early morning desert chill, but I was sweating in my windbreaker.

I parked the pickup thirty feet off the road, and then Kathy and I trotted up the road to take a position behind a clump of rocks where we could watch the house through the night-scope on the AR-15. It was a big, rambling two-story building, Spanish-style, with standard stucco walls a foot thick. The roof was tile. Kathy's diagram estimated twelve rooms, and the structure in front of us could handle fifteen. One light burned on the second floor. Two more lights burned on the ground floor. The rest of the house was dark, as was the small house to the rear, which Kathy said was the servant's quarters. At the east end, some French doors opened out onto a swimming pool shaped like a peanut. Beyond the pool was a tennis court.

The front door was big enough to drive a truck through. There was a low hedge bordering the curved driveway, all the way to the gate. Three cars sat in the driveway—a Rolls-Royce Silver Shadow, a red BMW, and a Mercedes. Kathy identified the Rolls as Mrs. Mayhew's and the BMW as Latrice's. "The Mercedes could be Dr. Hunsaker's."

"Anything not there that should be?"

"Landis drives a Chrysler convertible. And Gunther used to keep a Jeep in the garage."

"How does the place look?"

"Massive. And a little seedier. If you're not around, things go to pot."

"I don't like Gunther."

"He's not your kind of guy."

The fence was seven feet tall, but several of the supporting pillars had crumbled away where the iron rods of the fence had joined the stucco. Beside the electronic gate for cars was a smaller gate for people. I handed the night-scope to Kathy and spent a couple of minutes checking the guns and the plastique. I loaded the stun gun with a dart, and then I went back to the pickup for the aluminum ladder.

When I got back, breathing hard, Kathy handed me the night-scope. "There's someone."

I took the scope. A man was moving from the house to the Rolls, checking doors. He had some kind of automatic weapon slung over his shoulder. He moved slowly, as if he was half asleep.

"Know him?"

"He's big enough to be Willard."

"Who's Willard?"

"The bartender at Casere's."

"The big guy?"

"Yes. Mrs. Mayhew liked having him around because he fancied Landis and not the girls."

"How well does he know you?"

"All women look the same to Willard."

"Can you get him facing the main gate?"

"Call to him, you mean?"

"Yeah. Tell him your car's broken down. You need to use the phone."

"All right. Where will you be?"

"Coming up behind him."

I rechecked the stun gun. It's built like a sawed-off shotgun, and the darts are supposed to knock out the target for three hours. Stun guns were developed for use on animals. I hoped it had enough punch to handle Willard.

"I'm afraid, Matt."

"Good—healthy feeling." I handed over the keys to the Ford. "If anything happens to me, take the money and run."

"Oh, no. I—"

"I can shoot my way out, and I've been here before. This is for your daughter."

"For Lisa."

"Yeah. For Lisa."

Kathy brushed me lightly with her lips and then headed for the main gate. I carried the aluminum stepladder to the fence, leaned it against a stucco post, and shoved the rucksack through. I climbed up and dropped down, trying to keep it quiet. The grass was stiff and dry as winter. I had just started crawling toward the main gate when a hidden timer activated a bank of sprinklers on this side of the driveway from the fence to the house. The water misted up almost to eye level, wetting me down. I cursed as I trotted along the fence, staying low.

It was still dark, but a faint blue glow had appeared on the eastern horizon. Up ahead, I could see Willard's flashlight playing along his part of the fence. When he was almost to the gate, he stopped while he lifted his arms into the air for a stretch, and the flashlight pointed up at the fading stars. Willard was sleepy. I could almost hear his weary yawn. I bellied down on the wet grass and moved to the scraggly hedge, getting wetter every minute, until Willard was twenty feet away.

I waited until I heard Kathy call. "Yoo-hoo? Is anyone there? Yoo-hoo?"

"Who's that?" Willard swung around to face the gate. Even through the night-scope, his shoulders were huge. I figured his weight at two seventy-five.

"My car broke down on the road," Kathy said. "I need to use your phone to call for a tow truck or something."

"This is private property out here. Didn't you read the signs?"

"I know. I'm sorry. I got lost and then I hit one of those chuckholes and now my car won't—"

I was up and moving as Willard peered through the gate. "Hey? Don't I know—"

The stun gun was out, and my Nikes seemed slow and heavy in the wet grass. Kathy's face was vaguely visible through the fence in the beam of Willard's flashlight and Willard was a huge mountain in front of me, holding his Uzi muzzle down and starting to swing around just as he sensed someone coming, and then as he turned and started to train the Uzi on me, I hit him with a dart. The stun gun went *ker-chug* and there was a long moment where I thought the dope wasn't working, and then he crumpled to the asphalt, still clutching the Uzi, with the dart in his thigh.

When I made sure he was out, I searched his pockets. There were three sets of keys. One had a tag that said HOUSE. One said ROLLS. One said GATE AND GROUNDS. A key on the third ring opened the small gate. Kathy came through, clutching the Diamondback.

"I don't think I could use this on a . . . real person."

"I thought you wanted to waste Mrs. Mayhew."

She shook her head. "It's not like the movies, is it? I was scared to death. Frozen."

"You did just fine."

We dragged Willard behind the hedge, wired his hands and feet, and stuffed a sock in his mouth. The blue line on the horizon was turning white now as Sunday morning dawned. While Kathy stood guard, teeth chattering from fear, I wired the three cars with Zeke's plastique. The Rolls was set to go in ten minutes, the BMW in ten and a half, the Mercedes in fifteen.

"Why the different times?" Kathy whispered.

"Just a tactical move. The first one shakes them awake. The second one makes them know you're serious. The third one cuts off all thoughts of escape."

"You're a rascal, Matt."

"I have no idea whether it'll work."

She grabbed my arm. "You haven't tried it before?"

"I always wanted to."

"Dear God."

"Let's find that money."

On the way inside, I slid the Uzi into the swimming pool. The French doors opened with a gold key, and we stepped inside. The big house felt asleep. There was a short, stocky guy in a white coat snoozing in front of a bank of TV screens near the front door. A shoulder holster bulged under his white coat. Two of the TV screens were blank. The screen farthest to the left had a view of the gate, but Willard was not visible behind his hedge.

I hit the stocky guy with a dart, and he slumped down

in his chair with a soft grunt. I kept Kathy with me while we checked out the downstairs. It took two minutes and forty seconds. The kitchen was huge, done with white tile and stainless steel. No one was up and about.

We had eight minutes before the Rolls blew up. I took the stairs two at a time, on full alert. Kathy was behind me several steps. When she caught up, I pointed to the location of the master bedroom she'd drawn on motel stationery, and she pointed to our left and I nodded. Moving quickly now, we checked the rooms to our right. They were empty. The furniture was covered with sheets. We had six minutes before the first explosion. The first room to the left of the stairs was being used, but the bed was empty.

"Landis sleeps here," Kathy whispered.

We kept checking. Latrice's stuff was in the room next to the end. The secret door was stuck. It wouldn't open without a lot of noise, so we went back into the corridor. And in the master bedroom at the far end of the corridor, looking east toward a low range of hills and the white light that was edging the sky, we found two people sleeping. The room was huge. Two walls were lined with bookshelves. There was a Jacuzzi steaming in one corner, a writing desk, and two easy chairs. The windows were leaded glass. They gave the room a medieval feeling.

The bed was round and topped with a canopy and an overhead mirror. The closet doors—four of them— swung on hinges instead of rolling on plastic sliders. Quietly, I put Kathy into the first closet with the Diamondback and eased the heavy wooden door until it was almost closed. Then I slung the AR-15 and pulled out the .357 and flipped on the lights.

Mrs. Landis Mayhew raised up on one elbow, shielding

her eyes with one hand. She wore a pale gold negligee and she looked angry.

"Did you find—?"

She saw the gun and recognized me at the same time. Her pale eyes traveled up to my face. Her bedroom companion was a man with white hair who was about her age, but who lacked her mystical secret for staying young forever. So much for conventional medicine. Dr. Hunsaker moaned, rolled over, and pulled the covers over his head. Mrs. Mayhew glared at him, then at me.

"What is it, Mr. Murdock?"

I checked my watch. Five minutes before the Rolls blew. "Money."

"You're joking."

"It's for Kathy."

"She brought you here?"

"Drew me a good map."

"The money's not here. I can take you to it." She looked around the room, trying to adjust to her new situation. "You practically destroyed us, you know. Dashed our hopes and dreams, battered everything we'd built over the years."

"It was coming apart already, even before Hennessy's body turned up. You're slowing down, or you would have seen the signs."

She turned to Hunsaker and jerked the bed covers off. "Wake up, Judson. We have company."

Hunsaker grunted, opened one eye, saw me, and shuddered. He pulled the covers over his head again. Mrs. Mayhew gave me a pained expression. When she leaned forward to reach her gold silk wrapper, the front of her negligee fell open and she looked up at me and summoned up her best smile. Her eyes were smoky, a neat trick at that hour of the morning, and I saw why she'd gone into the world's oldest profession. Sexy at fifty-seven. "I'd love a little chat with Katherine. Can you take me to her?"

"Not today."

"Letting you run her little errand, I see." Mrs. Mayhew took her time putting on the wrapper. With it on, she looked even more undressed. Another cute trick.

"Kathy says you owe her two hundred thousand."

"Katherine's a liar. She's been conspiring for a year at least with that Jancey Sheridan to wrest control from me." Mrs. Mayhew started to climb out of bed, then decided against it and leaned back against her golden pillows.

I walked to the bed, prodded Hunsaker with the muzzle of the .357. "Get up, doc."

Hunsaker stuck his head out and glared at me before sitting up. His arms were starting to get stringy and he was working on a paunch that didn't show when he wore his doctor suit. I tossed him a pair of Brooks Brothers boxers. "I feel awful," he said. "My poor head."

"What was that stuff you were going to shoot me with, doc? The other night? In the hospital."

"Medication merely. A common sedative."

"You're a lousy liar, doc."

"And you're a typical paranoid." He stared at the gun muzzle and licked his lips.

I secured Hunsaker's hands behind him with wire. Wire works best because you don't need much and you can use hognose pliers. I sat him on the floor, with his back against the bed. Then I wired up Mrs. Mayhew. When I started poking through their luggage, Mrs. Mayhew spoke from the bed. "You're on the wrong side, Mr. Murdock. As well as on the wrong track, cosmically."

I opened a soft leather attaché case. Inside was currency—Swiss francs, German marks, Japanese yen, and U.S. greenbacks. I tossed the case onto the floor near the door.

"How's that?"

"Katherine's in league with a man, a European, in what could be construed as a corporate takeover of Lido Enterprises. I've been fighting them. That's why I wanted to hire you. Yet, like a fool, you played into their hands."

My watch said two minutes to the first explosion. I kept searching through the luggage as Mrs. Mayhew talked, and I hoped Kathy was getting a chuckle from her hiding place in the closet.

"Katherine's the archetypal slut," Mrs. Mayhew said. "At thirty-four, she can still transform herself into the vestal virgin of the village. Oh, I taught her some things, but that simple, ever-so-charming innocence of the girl next door is her own gift. I might say that she has developed it with all the guile of a serpent in the Garden of Eden."

"I thought that serpent was a boy."

"Bravo. Katherine thinks like a man."

It was almost time to bring Kathy out for the big finale. We had the money. The Rolls would blow in less than a minute. We could leave in a blaze of cars and Arab gasoline.

"Yes," Mrs. Mayhew hissed. "A snake in the grass. This man, this European who helped establish us with his capital, he fell under Katherine's spell. When he did, they began to bleed the operation of capital, which he took to Switzerland. At the same time, and at her insistence, he widened the scope of criminal activities to include illicit drugs. As you can imagine, I fought back. We are in the pleasure business, Mr. Murdock. Lido Enterprises will have nothing to do with controlled substances. It's wicked and goes against the higher laws. Yet in the last year, Katherine and her coconspirator have succeeded in marketing drugs worth seven million dollars."

"Crazy," I said.

"Take the Hennessy matter." Mrs. Mayhew's voice was cranked up to fishwife-shrill. "It has been established that his death was attributable to drugs, cocaine to be precise, and—you have guessed this, I am sure—Katherine was his source."

I hadn't found any more loot and I didn't have time to count what was in the briefcase. I walked around to Mrs. Mayhew's side of the bed and looked at her as she kept on with the crazy talk. "You're a fool. She's blinded you, and you're not the first by any means."

"Nice try."

"Katherine was with Edward Hennessy when he died."

"Bullshit."

"And I am working closely with Agent Dorn."

"Very funny." I made one more turn of the wire with the pliers. It was time to go. The AR-15 was slung over my right shoulder. I thought I heard movement on the lower floor. I put the pliers back in my pocket.

"Damn you to hell!" Mrs. Mayhew hissed. "Don't you see? Dorn and myself—against Katherine and the European!"

Thirty seconds before the Rolls blew. I was ready to bring Kathy out for a sweet good-bye. I didn't believe Mrs. Mayhew, but it was an interesting theory. "A for effort, Mrs. Mayhew. You and Dorn would make a swell team."

I heard a hiss from the doorway. And then Dorn's voice.

"Okay, hot dog. Turn around real slowly, no fast movements. Toss the revolver first, and then unsling that rifle."

I turned around. Dorn stood in the doorway, with Latrice. Instead of his three-piece, he wore slacks and a tan shirt with a necktie and a windbreaker. He still looked spiffy. Latrice wore a dark blue jumpsuit, reminiscent of British commando battle dress. She carried a Uzi. Dorn wielded a .357.

"Did you find him?" Mrs. Mayhew asked. "Did you find Landis?"

"Gone." Latrice shook her head. "Skipped the country, we fear."

The bed was between me and the doorway.

"Get me out of this wire," Mrs. Mayhew held up her wrists. "And be quick."

"You look all trussed up, Angie."

Mrs. Mayhew cut her eyes at Latrice. "What?"

With a wicked gleaming smile, Latrice hefted the Uzi, aiming first at me, then swinging it over a couple of inches to cover Mrs. Mayhew. "Don't point that thing at—"

"It's that time, Angie. It's—"

Then the Rolls exploded. The master bedroom was at the rear of the house, but you could see a corner of the driveway from here. There was a loud blast and a puff of brown smoke rolled across the swimming pool and I dropped down behind the bed and the Uzi went *spfffft* and while I was unslinging the AR-15, I heard Kathy's

Diamondback fire twice, followed by another handgun in reply, and then I was around the end of the bed, firing bursts at the doorway.

Dorn was not visible. Latrice was on one knee, spraying the room with automatic fire. I shot at her and missed, but the rounds were close enough to drive her backward, out into the corridor. We had ten seconds of silence while I listened and tried to figure my next move. I didn't know how Kathy was. Then I heard footsteps going away. I bellied around the bed to the corridor. When I looked around the corner over the AR-15, I saw Latrice turning a corner and heading for the stairs. I fired one round, but she was already down the stairs.

Then the BMW blew.

Mrs. Mayhew was slumped over in bed. She could wait. The wood on the closet door was ripped with lead. "Kathy? It's Matt. You okay?"

I could barely hear her answer.

"Don't shoot, kid! It's Matt!"

"Matt?" Her voice was faint and far away as I coaxed her out. Her face was pale. The sweater was ripped in her upper arm and blood was oozing out. She was holding the Diamondback in both hands. "Oh, Matt."

Outside, I heard the screech of tires on rubber as Latrice or Dorn or maybe both made their getaway. "How bad are you hit?"

She stared at me. "Hit? I don't feel a thing."

"Where's the arnica?"

"In my left pocket."

I got out the bottle and shook five pellets into Kathy's mouth. She nodded at me and then we checked Mrs. Mayhew. "Oh, no."

Mrs. Mayhew lay tilted over in the bed, her mouth

open, her eyes glazed over. There was a line of bullets stitched across her midsection from her right hipbone across her breasts to her left shoulder.

"Where's Hunsaker?"

We found the doctor under the bed. His eyes were wide open. He was about to shake to pieces. I needed his Mercedes. The pickup was too far away. "Where are your car keys, doc?"

"Over the—th . . ." He used his chin to guide me to his pants pockets, where I found the keys. I figured we had two minutes before the Mercedes blew up. "Don't leave me! All this death! Please don't leave me!"

We left him there with his wrists wired and hurried out the corridor. Kathy was crying. I carried the money bag.

Downstairs, the short guy in the white jacket was still out. The front door was open and you could smell rubber burning.

"Let's go!" Kathy urged. "Let's get away from here."

I handed her the money bag and rolled underneath the Mercedes and pulled the plastique out from beneath the rear bumper. I removed the timing mechanism and tossed the plastique into the rear seat and shoved Kathy into the passenger seat. "Got your keys to the Ford?"

"You're going after them, aren't you?"

The Mercedes started right away. "Meet me at the Holiday Inn in Palm Springs. Two weeks from today."

"You're crazy! We have the money!" She shook the leather bag at me. "We have what we came for!"

The electronic gate stood open.

We were out of the driveway now, forty yards from the Ford. "Hope you can drive a stick."

"Let them go, Matt! Let them go."

I had one clip left for the AR-15 and two speed-loaders

for the .357. The shotgun was still in the pickup. If I stopped for it, Dorn and Latrice would increase their lead. I figured they'd head west, toward Los Angeles and LAX. If I guessed wrong, they'd get away and Dorn would alert his people and . . .

No more ifs.

I wanted one more crack at them. I wheeled to a stop and told Kathy good luck.

"Matt!" she cried.

And then she was out of the car with the leather bag full of money and I was winding the Mercedes up and trying to evade the chuckholes in Gunther's private road as I headed north, toward Palm Springs.

15

By the time I made it onto Interstate 10, heading west, the light was desert gray. There was not much traffic on the road, two RVs going east, a Mayflower van going west. I cranked the Mercedes up past a hundred, a hundred and five, a hundred and ten. I passed a cowboy driving a pickup and three kids in a yellow VW with a surfboard mounted on the roof. The highway was straight and smooth. If I didn't sight Dorn and Latrice in fifteen minutes, they were gone.

At six-twenty, with the sun creeping over the horizon behind me, I saw a car barreling along a half mile ahead. My speedometer was at 115 and Hunsaker's big Mercedes seemed to float across the desert. Highway signs announced the Riverside turnoff, ten miles away. I kept the accelerator on the floor so I could get closer. The speeding vehicle was Dorn's tan sedan. Dorn was driving.

When the nose of the Mercedes was even with the rear bumper of the sedan, I rolled down the automatic window and laid the muzzle of the AR-15 on the window ledge and fired a burst at the sedan. The rear window shattered, and I zigzagged as I eased the Mercedes back just as Latrice leaned over the front seat and blasted me. Bullets slapped the door of the Mercedes. My rear window exploded. There was an exit sign up ahead, and an off-ramp heading north. I zoomed close again and banged into the tan sedan, hearing metal crunch as I rammed it onto the shoulder.

The impact sent the Mercedes reeling to the left lane. By the time I got her under control again, Dorn was taking the exit ramp. My momentum almost carried me past the ramp. I braked and swerved on. When I reached the top of the ramp, I spotted the sedan fifty yards ahead, heading north, toward a new development called Flute Hills. WELCOME TO FLUTE HILLS, the signs announced. RETIREMENT CONDOS FROM $99,595.

The right front tire of the Mercedes hit a chuckhole and I almost lost control. I was driving too fast and I felt crazy. An early biker on a red ten-speed saw me coming and pulled off the street onto a sidewalk. He gave me the Italian peace sign as I whipped through a stop sign at a four-way intersection, checking for the local law. I saw the tan sedan forty yards ahead where the road curved around the Flute Hills development, marked by the skeletons of half-finished buildings marching up along a ridge sculpted by bulldozer blades.

Steam was spitting in a thin stream from beneath the hood of the Mercedes when I caught up with them on a sharp curve, pulled wide into the left lane, cut my wheels, and tried for a sideswipe. The tan sedan was a standard Chevrolet four-door. The Mercedes was heavier. Latrice fired at me again from the rear window as the cars crunched together and Dorn's sedan rocked onto the shoulder, then down into a shallow ditch. I thought they were out of commission for a minute, but then the sedan climbed up and charged across an open space, churning up gravel and dry dust. I didn't see what happened to the sedan because I was busy keeping the Mercedes from rolling.

I got the Mercedes stopped forty yards away and swung around in a tilting U-turn. Out of the corner of my eye, I saw the sedan nosed up against a temporary toolshed. The doors were open and Latrice and Dorn were climbing the hill toward the unfinished buildings. Latrice still carried the Uzi. Dorn carried a satchel about the size of an attaché case. Metal glinted in the sun. As I watched, Dorn stumbled and slid back down. Latrice paused long enough to try to take the satchel. Dorn jerked it away, got to his feet, and kept climbing.

I parked the Mercedes ten yards from the Chevy, climbed out, took a deep breath, and put the plastique and the timer into my windbreaker pocket. It felt like kid's modeling clay. The construction gravel was bone-dry. When I reached the man-made slope, there was no sign of Dorn and Latrice above me. I heard a shout, then a single gunshot.

As I started my climb, a blue station wagon pulled off the road, and the driver called to me. "Hey, what's up?"

"Call the cops!" I yelled.

The dirt was loose under my feet, typical for fast-lane California construction. The Flute Hills development was a tidy complex of two-story townhouses. The advertisements said patios, sun-rooms, passive solar, tennis courts, an adult life-style. My mouth was dry from the dust. I would have paid money for a drink of water, but the thermos was in the pickup, with Kathy.

I dug my toes into the scrabbly hillside and plowed forward. Dust tickled my nose. Before I reached the top, a horn went off as the tan sedan caught fire. I kept chugging and reached the top, breathing hard. I peeked over, saw a gray slab, a mudsill, and a townhouse half framed. Over to the right was a stack of timber. I ran for it, zigzagging. Gunfire ripped the wood, making splinters of the two-by-four studs. I fired back with the AR-15.

I thought I heard a siren, but then the sound faded. I crawled on my belly around the perimeter. The dust kicked up near my right foot, and I rolled to the left and snapped one shot at a shadow against the rafters of a half-finished building about fifty feet away.

Someone replied with a short burst, driving wood into the air. The shots had come from above. Latrice and Dorn were shooting down. That gave them the advantage.

I bellied my way to the other end of the two-by-fours, looked around, and saw a flicker of movement on the second story of the building. I clocked the movements, took careful aim, and fired one round. A piece of scrap lumber fell to the ground. Someone cursed. I saw hurried motion.

To my right, I saw a cluster of three buildings where the roofs were being shingled. The walls were covered with gray foam insulation. At the edge of the closest building, a body lay. I could see a black boot, covered with dust, and one blue pants leg with a stripe. Security guard?

Gathering my courage, I dashed toward the guard.

Dust kicked up behind me as I ran. I dove the last ten feet, landed on the guard, and scurried behind a pile of concrete blocks. The guard didn't move. On his sleeve, a stitched gold shield read COCHRAN SECURITY AND ALARM. He was a young guy in his late twenties, with a round face and sideburns. His eyes stared out at nothing. Blood oozed from a wound in his throat. Bullets crashed around me. I fired back, emptying the AR-15, then pulled out the .357.

A voice called out: "Murdock?"

I didn't answer. The voice had seemed to come from a two-story condo sixty feet away and to my left. No movement. Except for the horns down below, not a sound. Now Latrice called from a different angle: "Murdock. Don't be stupid, mon. Let's make a deal."

"We'll split with you, Murdock. There's two hundred grand here. You get a third."

I fired two shots, one at Dorn, the other at Latrice, then I doubled back around the building, tripped, hit the ground, and felt a muscle tear in my right leg.

Now, from down below, I thought I heard tires on the gravel and the sound of a car door slamming. I hoped it was the cops. When I tried to move, the leg collapsed under me. Biting my lip, I crawled across a rough concrete slab.

I tuned into the Top Kick's instinct and could feel them closing in on me in a pincer movement. A step creaked on a wooden stair. I heard a loose board clatter through to the ground floor and hit with an empty sound. The sun was throwing long grainy shadows now and the desert mists were rising. I set the timer on the plastique for ninety seconds and packed the explosive against a stack of shingles. I crawled a dozen feet and waited in shadow next to some drywall. Maybe I could get one of them. In my mind, I saw a platoon of highway patrol officers and sheriff's deputies drinking coffee at an anonymous Denny's back up the road. While I died, they were cracking jokes and replaying their last in-service football game.

Bullets ripped into some floor joists above my head. I lifted the .357. Then someone fired from the other side, near the plastique and the shingles. Only this time, the bullets tore up the boards four feet away from where I sat. I scuttled sideways, but couldn't see either Dorn or Latrice. Then Dorn spoke from my right. I hoped he didn't see the plastique.

"Drop it, Murdock."

I froze and slowly turned my head. Dorn was off to my right, looking smug, holding the leather satchel in one hand and his chrome-plated pistol in the other. His face was streaked with dirt. His windbreaker looked mussed. How long before the plastique blows? Twenty seconds? Fifteen?

"Don't try it, Murdock."

"It was you," I said. "You fingered me in the hospital."

"Good thinking."

"I thought it was Hunsaker."

"Hunsaker couldn't finger his nose if it itched. Put down the piece."

I laid the .357 on the floor. My leg was cramping. "You're a mole, aren't you?"

"Try 'entrepreneur.' Always seeking opportunity."

"And you work for Mr. Big."

"Who's Mr. Big?"

"Gunther, the shadowy European. Lives in Brussels. Controls all the Swiss bank accounts."

"She told you, that—!"

Just as Dorn fired, I rolled clumsily to the left, grabbing for my .357, and I heard two explosions. The first one sounded like a shotgun. The second was my plastique, which blew shingles into the air near where Dorn stood, spinning him around. His second shot went wild.

My hand found the .357, and I scooted sideways to the edge of the building, where I crawled along the foundation. When I came to the corner, I saw Dorn sitting in the dirt, holding one hand around a wood splinter driven into his shoulder. The shotgun went off again. I left Dorn and bellied around another corner. Forty feet away, behind a pile of cement sacks, Kathy Kagle was firing my shotgun at Latrice, who was retreating to a dark doorway as she raked the area with her Uzi. I aimed at Latrice with both hands and squeezed off a round. She sagged, almost dropped the Uzi, then turned and vanished into the building behind her.

"Kathy? You okay?"

Her voice quavered. "Yes."

"Stay down!"

"Matt! Don't—!"

I caught a glimpse of Kathy as I limped after Latrice. I reached the stairs. The leg felt ready to explode under me. The green wood creaked as I took the stairs, hauling myself up, taking a splinter in the palm, one more in the finger. At the top of the stairs, I saw a shadow through the studs. I crawled around the corner. Latrice sat on the floor, braced up by the wall, left knee up, her right foot out in front. One sleeve of her blue jumpsuit was shredded. When I appeared, she fired a short burst from the Uzi, tearing the wood near my eyes. I hugged the floor and got off one shot that missed. As I reloaded, Latrice slithered out of sight, leaving a thin trail of blood.

She cursed me. "Motherfucker!"

I lay there, gasping for air. She reached a door at the end, turned right, and caught her sleeve on a nail. I fired and rolled, hearing the rounds from the Uzi claw the air above me, and then I came to a prone shooting position, elbows on the floor to prop up the .357, and shot Latrice. The bullet slammed her high in the shoulder. The Uzi fell and Latrice sagged against the drywall. I crawled toward her, finger on the trigger, and put the muzzle of the .357 against her cheek.

Her eyes narrowed, a snake ready to strike.

"Who was with you in the hospital?"

"Amateurs!" She coughed, but her eyes still blazed with hate.

"Why did you come for me there?"

She waited before answering. "Amateurs . . . need training."

"Who were the amateurs?"

She swiveled beneath me and came around with a knife in her long fingers. I slapped at the knife with the .357, knocking it out of reach, and on the return trip I clipped her cheek with the muzzle. Her head snapped back and she went limp on the floor. I stuck the muzzle of the gun in her ear.

"Names! I want their names! Whose idea was it to shoot up my house? Who are you? Names—!"

I didn't know how long I kept shouting, but one minute I was alone with Latrice and my need to know and the next minute there was someone else with us. It was a deputy in police suntans. He had a wide Irish face and eyebrows like Eddie Hennessy in the photo on the desk back in peaceful Irvine. The deputy had my gun and his gun. His mouth was moving, but I didn't understand him because I was shouting inside.

It took them forever to get us down and into ambulances. Kathy was not behind the cement sacks, where I had last seen her. There was no sign of the shotgun, but a young rookie cop found three empty 12-gauge casings. As they were helping me down the hill, I saw them putting Dorn into an ambulance. I didn't know whether he was alive or not. The ambulance drove away with its siren moaning. I thought about stopping to look for his attaché case, but I needed all my concentration to get down the hill. Maybe Kathy had picked it up.

Down below, a knot of cars had gathered and people stood behind a police barrier. Two men were spraying the smoldering sedan with red fire extinguishers. The Ford pickup was there, but Hunsaker's Mercedes was gone. Latrice glared at me as they trundled her into the ambulance.

I turned to my deputy. His name was Callahan. "Is Dorn alive?"

"Who?"

"The guy in the windbreaker."

"We're not allowed to give out that information."

"He usually wears a three-piece suit. Very snappy dresser."

"You always talk crazy?" Callahan asked.

"What about the woman?"

He laughed a short laugh. "You call that a woman?" He nodded at the departing ambulance.

"Maybe I was seeing things."

Callahan swung his big head around. "You guys from L.A. are all alike, know what I mean? It's from living too long with fags and colored. Live next door to your own kind is what I say. My daddy come out here from Pennsylvania to work defense. He lived in L.A. with them minorities before he got smart and up and moved the family here. Let 'em have the city is what I say. Shit, I won't even go in for a ball game no more. Better to catch it on the TV."

"It is nice here. A little warm."

"Shit. You call this warm? Wait 'til September! I'll show you warm."

At the hospital in Palm Springs, they gave me a shot for my leg and the muscle stopped twitching. Callahan stood outside my door, to ward off media people and keep the desert safe. A nurse cleaned up my shoulder and put on a fresh dressing. The resident who checked me out was amazed at how fast the gunshot wound was healing.

"When did you say you got shot?"

"Friday."

"Last Friday?"

"Yes. Why?"

"You're a fast healer, mister. This hole is knitting up like Luke Skywalker, and you'll be able to use the arm in a couple of days."

I didn't tell him I'd already used the arm. I didn't tell him about arnica. Or Kathy. Kathy had introduced me to arnica. Kathy had showed up at Flute Hills like the cavalry. Kathy had run out on me. Kathy would meet me in two weeks at the Holiday Inn.

Ha-ha.

I asked them to let me go. They smiled superior smiles. I talked first to a sheriff, second to a Palm Springs police lieutenant, and third to a young guy in chinos and an Abercrombie & Fitch windbreaker who was with the

CHP. I told them all to call Webby Smith in Laguna. My plan was to make Webby famous.

I was dozing when Webby arrived, wearing his uniform and looking grumpy. The time was around eleven. He handed me a cup of hospital coffee.

"Let's make a deal, Shamus."

"Okay." I was tired. I still hadn't found Hennessy's coins. I was worried about Kathy.

"You give me everything you got about Lido Enterprises and I'll get you out of here."

"Can I get out of here first?"

Webby squinted at me. "Too easy. You said that too easy."

"Let me guess what's up, Iron Man. With Dorn out, you're sitting pretty with the task force. With what I know about Lido Enterprises, you can make a name for yourself in law enforcement circles and retire famous. They'll want you in Hollywood, like that New York cop who became a movie star. I forget his name. I can see the name Webster Smith in lights on the big marquee."

"Finished with the speech?"

"Yeah."

"I'm the only man in the world can get you out of here."

"I appreciate that."

"Everyone else wants to make you the next Birdman of Alcatraz."

"I could use a cold beer."

"After."

"Is Dorn alive?"

"Still in surgery. They say he's got a wooden construction stake in his heart. They're calling him Agent Vampire."

"It's a piece of shingle. In the shoulder."

"How'd it get there?"

"Cosmic turn of events and a lucky charge of plastique."

"I thought you quit messing with that stuff."

"Did you figure out he's a mole? Did you figure out he works for Mr. Big?"

"Mr. Big is what we want to know about, Shamus."

"Okay, Mr. Big owns a safe house. It's south of Palm Springs, 7.6 miles. Electronic gate, couple of guards. There's a corpse up there and a shook-up doctor named Hunsaker and two security guards who will be coming to by the time you get there."

Webby picked up the phone and made three quick calls. I wasn't paying much attention about who he talked to. It was police business now. Let the police handle their business. The coffee tasted bitter. According to Kathy, coffee would antidote the arnica. What would antidote the coffee? What would antidote Mr. Big? Where was Kathy?

Webby hurried out cursing and the door closed. An orderly brought me thin soup and crackers and Jell-O. Callahan was still outside, guarding my door. Webby came back at two-thirty. He was grinning with partially fulfilled ambition.

"Goddamn, Shamus. Two hoods were leaving as we drove in. Both of them have records. Poor old Doc Hunsaker was chattering away. He calmed down after they gave him a sedative, and we think he'll turn state's evidence. Who did the job on the lady in the gold wrapper?"

"Latrice."

"The black woman in battle dress?"

"Yeah."

"They've named her Madame Slink." Webby shook his head. "How'd you know she did it?"

"Eyewitness."

"Will you swear to that in court? I know how shy you are. How you shun publicity."

"Do I get out of here?"

"Will you swear to swear?"

I smiled. "Yeah."

Webby helped me get dressed, and then we drove home in a police cruiser while I talked into a tape recorder about Lido Enterprises. When we were on Highway 55, Webby shut off the machine.

"Couple of other loose ends."

"Shoot."

"The shotgun was in your Ford. But the three casings were up behind some cement sacks. The deputy who brought you down didn't bring a shotgun. And Hunsaker says there was a woman with you. She had brown hair, good teeth, and a handsome figure. He says she worked for Lido Enterprises as a trainer-manager. Kagle, her name was. Katherine Kagle."

"She good with a shotgun?"

"You're evading again."

"Hunsaker's seeing things. He tried to jab me with a hypo and I fought him off and he hasn't forgiven me. You never know what trip a doctor's on these days. They have access to all those drugs and shit. I'd bet he's hooked on something illegal."

Webby laughed. "There was a woman. With you, there always is."

"Leave her out of it."

"Hunsaker's talked to other cops."

"Yeah. But he was raving, right?"

"Yeah. Right. He was raving." Traffic was thick as we crossed the San Diego Freeway, heading south. "Why do I put up with you, Murdock?"

"Because I bring light and truth to a dark world."

"Yeah," Webby said, "and I still believe in Santa Claus."

16

By late afternoon on Sunday, we were back in Orange County and I had finished my analysis of the demise of Lido Enterprises. My knowledge was limited. My scenario had a few blank spots, but in the next two months, as the story broke across headlines, magazine covers, and television, I saw that legions of reporters and armies of police didn't do much better. And it took them longer than nine days.

This was my rendition:

Mr. Big ran the show. He was the designer, the creator. He jockeyed around the world, thinking and plotting and reading in the bathroom. He had a good eye for female beauty. He kept apartments in Paris, London, Tokyo, New York—all the big cities—and owned an estate outside Brussels and the run-down house in Palm Springs. He had numbered accounts in Zurich. There were sister organizations in Las Vegas, Los Angeles, the Bay Area, Phoenix, Dallas, and Houston. I did not know their names, but I guessed they were not called Lido Enterprises. Along with prostitution, Mr. Big was into drugs and blackmail. It was a juicy story. I left Kathy out. I gave Webby Smith enough detail to jump him across several authority rungs in the vast bureaucracy of Operation Clean Sweep.

"Lunch on me," Webby said, as he dropped me at Slavick's Garage, where I picked up the Plymouth. Then I drove to the Dorado Motel and got a room and a six-pack. I was asleep before the second beer was halfway gone.

I woke up at midnight, sweating, wondering where I was. Neon light filtered through the motel curtains. I sat up for an hour, drinking beer as I stared into the darkness. My Ford was somewhere in the desert near Palm Springs. My house needed major repairs. Kathy had vanished. And Eddie Hennessy's coins were still missing.

I couldn't sleep, so I got dressed and took a walk on the beach. I had one shot at the coins. A long shot.

Monday morning, I was up at seven. I bought a tan bush jacket at a beach shop and some wire at a hardware store next door. I strapped on a shoulder holster I keep in the trunk of the Plymouth. The shoulder holster contained an army .45. I bought coffee and Danish at Mom's Café on Coast Highway and headed south, toward EJH Designs.

There were guards at the gates, but I found a spot outside the fence where I could see Ratner's black Mercedes. I was there at eight-twenty. Ratner came out at nine-thirty, carrying two small suitcases. The easy way he swung them made them seem empty.

We took MacArthur southwest to Newport Centre,

where Ratner parked near the Sutter Bank. The time was three minutes to ten when Ratner got out, carrying both suitcases. He was dressed in his usual spit-and-polish style, a khaki suit with a natty uniform fit, a conservative tie, and the cordovans with the high polish. He paced nervously while he waited for the bank to open.

At ten, a uniformed guard unlocked the doors and Ratner was the first customer inside. I watched through the window as Ratner stopped at the manager's desk to shake hands. After some chitchat, the manager spoke to someone on a white telephone. Ratner kept up the salesman's smile while he followed a pretty blonde with memorable legs to the safety-deposit cubicle. When he emerged a few minutes later, both attaché cases swung with new weight. He nodded at the manager, smiled at the blonde, and stepped outdoors. I had the strong feeling Barney Ratner was leaving town.

When he set the luggage down so he could unlock the Mercedes, I came up behind him and shoved the muzzle of the .45 in his ribs. "Latrice says hello."

"You crazy sonofa—"

Thirty feet away, a mother in a pink sunsuit scolded her two blond kids. In case she looked this way, I had the gun tucked between Ratner and the car. He edged away from the gun, as if I had touched a sore spot on his back rib.

"Walk around to the passenger side."

We walked around and he opened the door. When I shoved him in, he tried to close the door on me, but I rapped his shoulder with the .45. While he dealt with the pain, I wrapped three coils of wire around his wrists. The suitcases now weighed twenty pounds each. I got in behind the wheel.

"Are you crazy?"

"Where do you live?"

"Spyglass Hill."

"Ocean view, I bet."

"Screw the view. I got a frigging plane to catch."

I grinned. "It may leave without you."

"Goddamn you. I'm a taxpayer. You'll rot in jail for this."

We drove through the August morning to Spyglass Hill, where I parked in the garage of a two-story house a block away from a house I'd built in the late seventies. Ratner's had a better view of the Pacific. The Kawasaki bike sat against the west wall. When the garage door was closed, I helped Ratner out and handed him one of the suitcases. The other one could stay in the car. We walked in through the kitchen. Dishes were piled in the sink. There were three sacks of garbage that needed taking out.

"Messy in here."

"The maid comes tomorrow."

We sat down next to a huge potted palm in the big living room with the regulation cathedral ceiling, the regulation desert-tone carpet, deep and thick. Ratner lived well. I pushed the suitcase at him.

"Open it."

"It's locked."

"Unlock it."

"Can't get the key."

I grabbed the lapel of his khaki suit and jerked him to the floor. He landed on his knees and the pain came up in his eyes. "Pocket," he said. "Righ—coat pocket."

I got the key for him. He was sweating as he opened

219

the case, to reveal rows and rows of gold coins. They were in sets of ten or twenty, encased in plastic.

"Stealing from the boss, Barney. Tsk-tsk."

"I was taking them back."

"Good for you."

"No shit. I caught the little secretary hauling them out. I fired her ass and put them away for safekeeping. I was all set to hand them over when you stuck a gun in my back."

He was pale under his tennis tan and he couldn't stop sweating.

"No sale." I jerked him to his feet and we headed upstairs.

"Swear to God, I'm telling the truth. The day after Eddie dies, I come in and find Dottie Baby grabbing the coins. I already suspect she's supplying him with blow. I tell her to split. I figure the cops will dig into the safe, so I tuck the coins away for a couple days."

"Honest Barney Ratner."

He stumbled on the stairs. "What do you want up here?"

"I'm gonna open a window and roll you off your roof."

"Goddamn you—!"

There were three bedrooms upstairs, plus a bonus room at the far end of the hall. The master bedroom was at the front of the house, with a $2 million ocean view. I wired Ratner to the four-poster bed while I went through his closet. In the back of the closet, I found a Ninja suit and a curved Ninja sword. The black blouse had a rip in the right side. I showed the stuff to Ratner.

"Latrice called you an amateur."

"Who's Latrice?"

"Mrs. Mayhew's Jamaican bodyguard. The karate

220

killer, the one who recruited an ex-Naval Intelligence hot dog for a raid on room 4019 at St. Boniface. You were just keeping in shape, weren't you? Just keeping your hand in?"

Ratner shook his head groggily. "Who's Mrs. Mayhew?"

"She runs Lido Enterprises."

"What's Lido Enterprises?"

"That's the outfit that supplied the girls for the SBEN. You know what the SBEN is?"

"Sure. I founded it. Me and Eddie. So what?"

Ratner needed motivating. In the bathroom, I found some scissors. His eyes got wide when I started snipping away at his khaki coat. I went up the back seam, dividing the coat in two parts. "You're crazier than I thought!"

I pushed the jacket halves aside and went after the shirt. Ratner squirmed as the tip of the scissors pushed against his bare skin. When the shirt was opened up, I saw what I was looking for—a bandage about four inches square on his back ribs above his kidney.

I touched it gently, and he flinched as if he'd been touched by a hot poker.

"Goddamn you!"

I snipped the wire and tossed him a clean shirt. "Let's hit the station. I want the cops to see the coins and the gunshot wound."

"Gunshot wound, my ass. I fell, riding the bike."

"Sure you did."

On the drive to the station, he tried to bribe me three times with the coins. He didn't tell me where he was going, but the plane ticket was for Mazatlán, down in Mexico.

I turned a trembling Barney Ratner over to Sergeant Book, along with one suitcase of coins and the Ninja

221

stuff. The coins had been reported stolen, so they could hold him for a while. He'd be out on bail in no time. Book did not come close to buying my version of the hospital hit.

"This is a prominent citizen, Murdock. He pays taxes. He has friends in high places."

"Yeah. And he has some gold coins belonging to his dead boss."

"Did you say you were emigrating to Australia?"

"No."

"Katmandu?"

"Too cold in Katmandu."

I left Ratner and his salesman's personality with the police. The sun was hot. The Plymouth was in a parking lot in Fashion Centre. The Ford was still in the desert. It was almost noon on Monday and I had the keys to Ratner's Mercedes. I drove in comfort to the Newport Pier. My house was padlocked and a police cruiser was parked downstairs. That's one reason I stopped being a cop—they go on alert after the shooting stops. I studied my house from the street and then had a long lunch at the Blue Beat, where a pitcher of beer and a hamburger gave me the strength for an inspection of the battle site.

The cop was named Kopecki. We walked upstairs and he opened the padlock. One of the hinges had been blown off the door, so it dragged. We pushed it open. Webby's brief report hadn't prepared me for the mess, the feeling of being physically hit. The windows were gone. There was a double track of bullet holes in the front door. My rack of coffee mugs was shattered. The TV screen was blown away. My answering machine would never speak again. The fridge had leaked onto the

222

about to say more, but shook her head, sat back against the sofa, and crossed her legs. She was wearing a white skirt with a slit up one side and a bright orange blouse with shoulder pads. The blouse had three buttons undone. She gave me a speculative look. "You're part owner of Daddy's boat, aren't you?"

"Yes."

"I'm thinking of keeping the boat. What do you think?"

"You're the majority stockholder. It's up to you."

"Daddy was always promising me a sail. But mother went into a snit every time he did. Would you like a drink? Something stronger?"

"I should be going, but thanks."

She looked disappointed, but then she brightened. "Another time, then?"

"Sure."

Lizzie Hennessy walked me to the car. She bumped my hip with hers, twice, a clear invitation. She put a hand on my arm. "I think I should explain, Mr. Murdock. I knew my folks weren't hitting it off in the bed department. Mother's old-fashioned. Those photos got to her. If it had been me, I'd have done something about myself. Daddy played tennis to stay in shape. She let herself go."

"So the photos didn't shock you?"

"No."

So much for protecting the innocent daughter. "Would you like me to go with you to the bank?"

"What for?"

"To lock those coins up."

"Oh, fun. Then you could take me to lunch after?"

"Sorry. I've got a house to build."

"Or I could take you to lunch. Mother must still owe you some money?"

"We're square."

"Well, would you drop me at the Talbots' on your way? I want to show the coins off."

"Sure."

Legs shining, she ran back to get the suitcase. The pickup amused her. The orange blouse stayed open and the slit in the skirt showed me a lot of her tan. She was putting herself on display. I like a display as much as the next guy, but Lizzie was embarrassing me. The drive took less than a minute before I braked in front of the Talbots'.

"Call me sometime. We'll take the boat out."

"Sure."

"You don't mean it, do you?"

"No."

"Bye."

As I pulled away, I saw her walking up to ring the bell at the Talbots' on Tamarack. The suitcase swung heavily. Tommy's Volvo was in the driveway. The garage was open. There was no sign of Midge's car.

Two days later, with the Lido Enterprises story dominating the news, I met Tommy Talbot for lunch. Tommy looked thin and harried. He picked at his food and kept ordering martinis. When I handed over the paper sack containing his blackmail tape, his eyebrows arched in a question. "What's this, partner?"

"The tape they had of you."

He shoved it out of sight and downed his martini. "How was I on camera?"

"I don't know. I didn't watch it."

"Do the police—?"

"Not as far as I know."

Tommy rolled the ice in his glass. "Midge is gone, partner. Left me high and dry."

It explained the all-martini lunch. "Oh?"

"Yeah. Flew out yesterday, back to Missouri. She was royally pissed, you might say."

"What tipped her?"

"A fluke. She rode to the hospital with Christie Hennessy, who couldn't shut her trap about Eddie and the hookers in those photos. Midge asked the right questions and put two and two together about Monday at the old SBEN and came up with my head on a platter. Call me John the Baptist. She wants half of everything, including the boat. Thank you, Christie Hennessy. I never liked her. Drinks too much. Fills the house with cigarette smoke. The daughter's a nice kid, though. Real head on her shoulders." Tommy stared at me like Midge's departure was my fault and signaled the waitress for a refill. "The house is for sale, but the market is down ten percent. The business is with a broker, but the bids are way too low. I haven't heard word one from my good SBEN buddies since all this happened. And I'm thinking of heading back to Barstow."

The wages of sin.

"Tommy, why didn't you tell me about Sally Anne?"

"The little hooker? Tell you what?"

"She worked for Lido Enterprises, pal. You knew that the day she went overboard. You made the connection with Mrs. Mayhew in the hospital. That's why you had a bellyache. You knew all that when you asked me for help."

Tommy clapped me on the shoulder, the old jock brotherhood grip. "Partner, you're like Hercules. You love cleaning the shit out of stables. It's your role, man.

Your role! Guys like you don't want to know too much! It ruins the sport."

"She was with Hennessy, Tommy. She was with him when he died. You thought you were protecting your ass by not telling me."

Tommy looked past me into the distance. "I wasn't Eddie's keeper. He took a risk. We all did."

"And you knew Hunsaker, didn't you? And that act at the hospital was pure bullshit."

"Jeez, don't yell." Tommy smiled as the waitress arrived with his martini. "Ah, here's the pretty lady with the refill. Hello, pretty lady! You free tonight? Because you are looking at one free—"

I grabbed Tommy's lapel. "I got your goddamn tape. I almost got killed doing it."

The waitress hurried away. Tommy watched her go. His eyes were red from too much martini. "Did I tell you I'm thinking of going back to Barstow? Considering going back home? Don't know what the hell I'll do when I get there, but—"

I shoved my chair back and stood up.

Tommy's smile was weak as water. "Can you spring for this, partner? My credit's busted."

I tossed twelve bills on the table, all hundreds. He picked up the money. He was counting it slowly as I walked out.

For the next ten days, the Lido Enterprises saga widened from Newport Beach to include Los Angeles, then San Francisco, then Phoenix and San Diego, then Portland, then Seattle, then Houston. Dr. Hunsaker was labeled "Dr. Clean" by the media because of his role in Mrs. Mayhew's organization. "Yes," the doctor said on television, "I was fully aware of the possible pathology involved, and that's why I made my services available. As a physician, I was able to maintain a strict control of the participants, and we fully expected our research to contribute in a significant way to the vast future of scientific knowledge." The newspapers, who view contradiction as a terrible sin, set Hunsaker's Lido Enterprises involvement up against his public image—noted physician, conservative Republican, church deacon, and yachtsman extraordinaire. He made good copy. But all around him you could sense the imminence of insanity, delusions of grandeur, the approaching nervous breakdown as he lost touch.

Hunsaker's public statement reminded me of that hypo he'd been so eager to give me, so I called Sergeant Book and asked what the lab boys had found.

"An arsenic derivative," Book said. "You calling from Katmandu or Outer Mongolia?"

"How deadly was it?"

"Take a small squirt to kill someone. But we don't know the perpetrator."

"Hunsaker."

"Hooray for you. We got this guy around the bend. No fingerprints. No motive. Just a dab of arsenic in a shattered hypodermic. I hear it snows early in Nepal. Watch out you don't get buried in a blizzard."

"Any news about Ratner?"

"No."

"Latrice? Dorn?"

"They're both in the prison ward. Every day, we need more guards to keep out the goddamn press. Good-bye."

Rumors about Latrice boosted newspaper circulation through September. A dozen big-name magazines with glossy covers offered her thousands for her exclusive tale.

In mid-September, Latrice was indicted for the murder of Mrs. Angela Mayhew. I got to testify on that one. They brought in a hot prosecutor from the DA's office. There were diagrams of Gunther's house, the hallway, the bedroom where Mrs. Mayhew had died. Ballistics tied the bullets that killed Mrs. Mayhew to Latrice's Uzi.

Latrice's newest nickname in the news media was Shadow Lady. The more the reporters dug, the less they knew. In the seared luggage in the tan sedan, the police found three fake passports bearing Latrice's photo. In the Swiss passport, her name was Geneviève Chambord. In the British passport, it was Amanda St. James. In the Egyptian passport, it was Aida Ryadhi. The luggage was Gucci. There was no American passport.

The *Times* and the *OC Tribune* sent reporters to Washington and Europe and North Africa to research Latrice. They came up with zero. Interpol had an open file on Aida Ryadhi, Latrice's third alias, but they had lost track of her a year ago in Brussels.

A day after Latrice was indicted, Agent Dorn issued a statement saying Latrice had killed Mrs. Mayhew on orders from Mr. Big. Dorn's story roughly paralleled the line of bullshit from Mrs. Mayhew—that they were working together to bring down a shadowy underworld figure who controlled a vast vice trade from a shadowy European headquarters. According to Dorn, Dr. Hunsaker was part of the governing committee of Lido Enterprises, a role larger than that of physician to the nightingales. Dorn's statement was issued from his sickbed in the prison ward at UC-Med in Orange. There was a photo showing him propped against the pillows as he was interviewed by reporters. That night, the eleven o'clock news ran a five-minute segment of the interview. Then an official from the DEA said the charges against Dorn might be reevaluated, because he had been so cooperative and apparently could be a valuable source against international crime. And there were essays in the newspaper praising him for his courage in going underground.

Sympathy was building for Dorn when a reporter from Las Vegas found a house on Bonanza Road worth $500,000 and a bank account with $450,000 in cash. Both were registered in the name of Dorn's brother, Vincent, who had died in Vietnam. Agent Dorn's stuff was in the house—thirty-seven snappy suits from Savile Row, and fifty-two pairs of handmade boots and shoes, and a hundred pairs of underwear still in the packages from Brooks Brothers. Dorn was executor of his brother's estate. His DEA salary had been $43,000 a year. His stamp collection was worth at least $5 million. Inquiries and offers about the collection bogged down the phone lines at the Las Vegas Police Department.

Then Doc Hunsaker called a press conference and accused Dorn of being a "mole" working for the shadowy European. According to Hunsaker, Dorn's assignment was troubleshooter. He was paid by the DEA, but his loyalty was to Mr. Big. His assignment in Southern California was to ferret out a blackmailer, one Jancey Sheridan by name, a small-time hoodlum from Arkansas.

No one paid much attention to Dr. Hunsaker. His Mr. Big theories were mixed in with ravings about plague and pestilence, about playgirls and angels of persuasion. Attendants on night duty at UC-Med said he ranted in his sleep and had nightmares about a woman in a ghostly white gown who he could identify only as Number 12.

The day after Latrice signed her exclusive contract with *Vertigo* magazine, police in Indio found the body of

Landis Mayhew. He had been buried in the desert in a shallow grave. Coyotes had dug him up. Birds had picked at him. There wasn't much left of the big blond man who had won some tennis matches in Paris in the seventies. The preliminary police report said Landis had died of multiple gunshot wounds. Most of the slugs were from an Uzi. Two were from Dorn's .357 Magnum.

Dorn denied killing Landis. Hunsaker took to the airwaves for one last time and accused Latrice and Dorn of ritual murder. They were instruments of the shadowy European, Hunsaker said. Latrice said both Dorn and Hunsaker were fools.

A few hours after Landis was discovered, Dorn died in his bed at UC-Med in Orange. The apparent cause of death was cardiac arrest. Hunsaker swore Dorn was killed by operatives of Mr. Big.

"That Doctor Clean," Latrice said on the five o'clock news, "he spent too much time with the madame. She was into her own voodoo. There is no Mr. Big. There never was."

You could hear Latrice snickering all the way from her cell.

17

In late September, I received a special custom postcard from Captain Tommy Talbot, postmarked Hawaii. The color photo showed the *Laredo II* against a fantasy backdrop of blue sea and white sky. Half a dozen people, wearing skimpily fashionable beach gear, sipped cocktails on the high-polish deck. One of the people was Captain Tommy, looking lean and fit in sailors' cutoffs and deck shoes with no socks. His face displayed only happiness, with no shadow of doubt about the endless good life. The girl beside him, with her rag-mop hairdo and a nothing yellow bikini, was Lizzie Hennessy. Lizzie was smiling smugly, like a girl who'd just inherited a bundle without working for it. Everyone on board looked rich, famous, relaxed, happy.

Dear Partner—

The days here are perfection—sunshine, just

enough breeze. The whiskey is sea-dog smooth.
Irvine house still for sale. Divorce proceeding. Liz
sends regards. On to Tahiti. Sure beats the hell out
of Barstow!

T. Talbot, Esq.

P.S. If you grow weary from cleaning those Augean
stables and all the shit of the world, Liz has a
<u>knockout</u> friend.

It seemed like we could keep the *Laredo II*, after all.
Maybe now I could sell my share.

By October, the Lido Enterprises story was old news
fading to the back page and my arm worked again with
only the occasional twinge and I was back in my house. I
had a new top on the kitchen cabinet, Mexican tile with a
blue border. The bullet holes had been plugged and the
walls shone brightly with a fresh coat of paint. All the
windows were in. I bought a four-year-old fridge out of
the classifieds. The former owners had sold it when the
ice maker refused to work. I fixed the ice maker, then
disconnected it. You can get too many gadgets.

In honor of the World Series, I bought a two-year-old
TV from a friend of a friend who was upgrading. It had
a twenty-five-inch screen and superior color, and it came
equipped with a remote control box that allowed you to
play network roulette without getting out of your chair.
The guy who invented remote control had us beer drink-
ers in mind. Punching the buttons from my chair
changed my opinion about too many gadgets. This was
control. This was survival. That year, we had a memorable World Series.

Webby Smith dropped by one evening to deliver some

guns—the AR-15, the .357, the shotgun, and Bongo's Walther—and to tell me he was flying back to Washington. I offered him a beer. He accepted with a sigh.

"Don't tell me, Iron Man. You've joined the FBI. You're going to guard the president when he visits the Ayatollah. They're giving you a medal."

"Hold your applause, please. Just a simple consulting job for D.C.'s finest. Seems there's a vice ring operating that looks like the clone of Lido Enterprises. They've got expensive call girls, executive drugs, blackmail videos, and connections with a group of high-salaried professional types called the KOP, Knights of the Potomac. They want me to show them how to keep the lid on."

"Any leads on Mr. Big?"

Webby shook his head and drank some Bud. "No one believes in Mr. Big except you, me, and Doc Hunsaker. Two big-time newspapers sent reporters to Europe. One was in a car crash. The other one came up empty. No Brussels estate. No apartments in Paris or Berlin or Rome. The DEA sent a top man over. He fell in love with a student at the Sorbonne. Officially, Mr. Big does not exist."

"Let me run him down, Webby. I'll free-lance for the task force."

"I brought your name up at a high-powered meeting the other day. They think you're too hot. Too much press exposure."

"Latrice knows something. You can tell by her smirk."

"Can't get to her through the goddamn writers and editors." Webby looked around at my repair work. "You've done a nice job fixing up after the shoot-out. Ever think about going back to honest work?"

"That's one good thing about exposure. I've got more business than I can handle."

Webby finished his beer, stood up, and slapped his stomach. "This lunch circuit is making me soft as cream cheese. You sit around this table with all these law enforcement guys smoking cigars and study papers and look at charts and the charts show these clones of Lido Enterprises springing up in St. Louis, Dallas, Kansas City, Chicago, and you wonder if it's all worth it."

"Fight the good fight, Iron Man."

"Where is the good fight?" Webby asked as he walked to the door. "God, do I feel old."

The first week in October, I received two referrals from the blue-chip lawyer J. Benton Sturges. The first case was a bodyguarding job in Beverly Hills that took a day. The second case was a hunt for a missing juvenile that took me down into Mexico for a week. Before I left, I bought a new answering machine, and when I came back with the juvenile in tow, there were lots of messages. Most of them were from potential clients who had read about me in the newspapers. One was a writer who wanted to do a chapter on me for a book he was writing called *The Vigilante Mind*. And one message kept repeating, drifting in between the others. It was a woman's voice, but the caller did not identify herself. The message was simple. "Holiday Inn, your name, Palm Springs. Holiday Inn, your name, Palm Springs."

I knew the voice. It sounded so close you could reach out and touch it, like the advertisement says. It was a whispery voice, soft, pleasant, soothing. A warm voice. A sexy voice. A voice to go to sleep by. It could have played on the radio in one of those after-midnight DJ shows where you ride around in the dark with the rain drifting down and you listen to this voice and it slips right through your ears to thump your heart.

So I listened to the voice on the tape again, and then I said "What the hell" and called Palm Springs and made a reservation. Today was Sunday. I made the reservation for Monday. She wanted it played her way. I wanted to see her. We'd play it her way.

Monday afternoon, I drove east on the Riverside Freeway to Interstate 10, and I was in Palm Springs by four o'clock. I checked in. The room was a double, with two queen-size beds and only the faintest trace of cigarette smoke. I had a swim and a shower. I watched the news. A police spokesman in Washington D.C. gave us viewers ninety seconds of bullshit. "On the alleged vice ring operating in the nation's capital, we have no information at this time. On the alleged existence of a special task force, which some have said resembles a similar force operating in California during the late summer, we have no information at this time."

Poor Webby.

The phone rang at seven.

"Hello."

"Matt?"

"Yes."

"I'm in the lobby. Can you meet me in the lounge?" Her voice still held warmth and sweet promise.

"Sure."

"It will be lovely to see you."

She was in the lounge when I arrived, sitting at a table overlooking the pool. She wore a green dress with a modest neckline and medium sleeves that showed her brown arms. Her hair was rich and lustrous. It was cut medium, in a style that accented her Nordic cheekbones. She wore sensible medium heels that made her legs look pretty. Her eyes lit up when she saw me enter the room, and you could feel the air go out of the bird dogs at the bar who'd been building their courage to go over and try to pick her up. I thought of Jancey's metaphor about bees and honey.

She stood up and we shook hands and my mouth got dry. She was drinking white wine. I ordered a beer. Her eyes were shining. She was very beautiful.

"How are you? How's the arm?"

I touched my left shoulder. "Okay. How's *your* arm?"

She nodded. "Fine. I hated to leave you there, Matt. But I heard your voice and it sounded like you were in control, so I scooted. They would have thrown me in jail, along with the others."

"Where did you get medical attention?"

"There was a doctor in Palm Springs, a—" She paused, smiled. "I started to say 'friend.' He was a customer. He patched me up and I stayed at his place a couple of days. The arnica worked wonders."

"I was worried."

"Thank you for that. Did you get your pickup back okay?"

I nodded. My beer arrived and I took a sip. Now that we were talking, it was like old times. This woman stirred me up. "How's your daughter? Lisa, right?"

"Um, Lisa. She's up and walking, taking lots of therapy. We're living together in Denver. I have a new name, new credit cards, everything. I paid a man five thousand dollars for a new identity—that's something I learned working for Mrs. Mayhew—but I'm not telling you the details. I hope you understand."

"Sure. What's in a name, anyway?"

"Did you get your house fixed up? After the shooting?"

"Come see for yourself."

Kathy looked around at the lounge. Across the room, a blonde in her twenties was laughing at a joke told by a man in a Hawaiian shirt. The blonde wore a low-cut red dress and had on too much makeup. The man had a wide mouth and a beer gut that he could not fully conceal with the shirt.

"I hope it was all right, meeting in the bar like this."

"No problem."

"I wanted to try it . . . a date, I mean. To see how it feels."

"How does it feel?"

She smiled and bit her lip. "Nervous."

"Want to talk about it?"

"Okay. My heart's beating fast. My palms are sweaty. I want to get up and run. Before you got here, I felt like a huge spotlight was beaming down on me. I felt the eyes of all those men, poking."

"Still feel that spotlight?"

"A little."

"What about a walk? It should be cool now."

She looked at me gratefully. "A walk would be lovely."

At first, walking along, we didn't touch. Then we turned a corner and our hips bumped nicely and Kathy took my hand. "You think everyone goes through this? The first date, I mean?"

"Yes."

"Do you?"

"Sure. I'm human. But this isn't our first date."

"You know what I mean." She jabbed my arm playfully. "Anyway, you don't look nervous. You never look nervous. Even when the bullets were flying, you were cool as an iceberg."

"I'm a guy. Guys can't."

"Why not?"

I thought about that a minute. "If you're a guy and you look nervous, you don't get hired. If you don't get hired, you lose your self-respect, because you get self-respect from working. If you lose your self-respect, then you're not a man anymore."

"Poor you. Poor men."

She snuggled into me. We walked along. When the big leather shoulder bag banged my hip, she shifted it to her other shoulder. After a while, she said, "I was never nervous as a hooker. I've been thinking about that a lot lately. As a hooker, I was in control. My emotions were turned off. My services had a good reputation. I could wheel and deal. I was a product on the marketplace, in demand, commanding premium prices. And I was constantly getting my small revenge."

"That sounds like a page from a book."

She squeezed my hand. "You knew, didn't you? You knew without my telling you. I'm writing it down, Matt. The whole sordid story."

"I had a feeling."

"It started one night when I couldn't sleep. I got out the journal and paged through it, and when the memories started to flow, I jotted down some notes. Once I filled a couple of yellow pads with notes, I bought a typewriter so I could type them up, and pretty soon I needed some organization so I fooled around with chapters and chapter titles—do you think I'm crazy?"

She glowed with excitement. "You going to try to publish it?"

"I think so. How about this title? *Confessions of a $1,000 Call Girl.*"

"You want to be careful it doesn't boomerang. Mr. Big wouldn't want egg on his face."

She was quiet for a moment. "I've covered that, I think. I'll get an agent and use a pseudonym—Zorah or Gwendolyn or Tamara—or just an initial like Z. I'll incorporate and get paid only in cash, and no one will know but you and the agent. It's risky, but it seems so right!" We walked along while I considered her plan.

"It might work."

She turned to me and put her arms around me and put her face up for a kiss.

"I have news, Mr. Detective."

"Tell me the news."

"I'm not nervous anymore."

"Good."

"And I'm so glad to see you!" Her arms tightened around me and I felt the pressure of hip and thigh.

"It's good to see you, too, Kathy."

"Please take me to your room, sir. And then take me. And while you are taking me, please say that word again in my ear."

"What word?"

"Illegal," she whispered.

We spent the night making love. When we needed a breather around midnight, we called room service and ordered breakfast. At three in the morning, after more love, we went for a moonlit swim. We came back to the room and took a long shower together and made more love, and I kept having the feeling she had come to say good-bye.

We had one last conversation.

"I've been wondering. Did you get Dorn's attaché case?"

There was a significant pause. "Yes."

"What was in it?"

"Not much. Twenty thousand in cash. Half is yours."

"No diamonds? No coke? No gold bullion? No stamp collection?"

"Sorry, dear. You want your half now?"

"Later." I reached for her. She smiled as she came into my arms. The smile was for me and no one else. I felt certain of that.

When I woke, the clock said three minutes after seven and Kathy was gone. There was a note for me on the motel dresser, along with a stack of hundred-dollar bills and a typed manuscript of her confessions. She hadn't said her book was finished. But it was, all four hundred pages of it.

The note was in Kathy's careful hand:

"Darling. Thanks for my first *real* date. I know it's not the last. Love, Kathy. P.S. The money is from Lisa. I told her a lovely man had helped me help her. She wants you to have it. I know you're proud. I know what you're thinking. Use it to fix up your lovely, lovely home. K."

There were a hundred bills, all hundreds.

Over breakfast in the motel coffee shop, I started reading Kathy's manuscript. The first line was a grabber: "My life as a thousand-dollar call girl began when I was raped at the age of seventeen. The rapist was a football hero from a prominent family. He was a bully—greedy, proud, stupid, and very strong. I fought him until he overpowered me, until I had no choice but to submit. I am still afraid of that man today. I am still afraid of his brothers, his cousins, his stupid macho pals. He is one reason I became a thousand-dollar call girl—so I could fight back."

I went back to the room and kept reading. The manuscript was neatly typed, with Kathy's notes to herself in the margins. The opening chapter, "Scenario," spelled out the dating process at Lido Enterprises. There was a lush description of the room at the Cote D'Azur, here called the Ritz Rialto, with the men in their business suits waiting for the arrival of the girls, and then the girls sweeping in. Kathy had given each girl a bird's name— Ms. Sparrow, Ms. Robin, Ms. Cockatoo, Ms. Hawke—and Mrs. Mayhew was called Madame Thrush.

The other chapters were a mixture of narrative, case studies, and the eternal mystery of sexual attraction. There was a heavy dose of Carl Jung in the chapter called "Anima Force" and a nice verbal picture of Arlene (aka Frieda Nightengale) in "The Substitution Game." The chapter on Mrs. Mayhew, "Beverly Thrush from Georgia," had a long section on Cassandra the Courtesan, the woman who had passed on the secret of eternal life to Mrs. Mayhew. She'd been a mistress to princes and dukes and generals and mobsters and bankers. My conclusion after reading about Cassandra was that prostitution would be around as long as there was civilization.

The last section was "Journey into Vice," which was Kathy's story, beginning with a stark picture of her lonely life, the rape, giving up her child for adoption, college, Arlene-Frieda, her first trick, Malibu, and her life with Mrs. Mayhew. She did a good job of placing Lido Enterprises in a large Sunbelt city and disguising people I recognized as Tommy and Eddie and Barney and Doc Hunsaker. I kept waiting for her to bring Mr. Big onstage—the suave European, the endless apartments, the Zurich bank accounts—but he didn't appear. I turned to the last page. I read "The End." The book was over. But the case wasn't.

So I lay there on my unmade bed in the Holiday Inn on the southern edge of the Mojave Desert, and I thought about what Mrs. Mayhew had said about Kathy and Mr. Big just before she had died. And then I remembered that Latrice had not mentioned Mr. Big in the first two installments of her exclusive life story that was running in *Vertigo*. Latrice had executed Mrs. Mayhew. And Dorn had worked for someone much higher up, and Kathy had come back to Flute Hills for Dorn's attaché case, because there was something in the case that higher-up someone wanted.

But that was only theory.

But if it was accurate, I now understood why Kathy could write her goddamn book. She'd been writing it all along. She'd been writing it with the blessings of Mr. Big, who toyed with people, who reshaped lives with money and power.

So that officially Mr. Big would not exist.

And Kathy's message to me was to leave Mr. Big alone. That's why she'd come to Palm Springs. That's why she had shown me the book, the neatly typed pages, the careful sentences, the thoughtful notes to herself in the margin. The Mayhew machine belonged to Mr. Big. It was his idea, his baby. By writing him out, Kathy bought herself a future.

I threw the manuscript on the floor. Papers flew. I'd bet money she wasn't living in Denver.

If I ever met the man, I'd kill him.

For a complete list of books available from Penguin in the United States, write to Dept. DG, Penguin Books, 299 Murray Hill Parkway, East Rutherford, New Jersey 07073.

For a complete list of books available from Penguin in Canada, write to Penguin Books Canada Limited, 2801 John Street, Markham, Ontario L3R 1B4.